Praise for
The
Free-Lance
Pallbearers

"A madly exuberant fantasy about a benevolent despot . . . suggests a psychedelic light show, fountains of words and images and hip argot. There is some Hieronymus Bosch brilliance in this free-wheeling prose."—*San Francisco Chronicle*

"Reed's feints are brilliant and his punches swift."—*Commonweal*

"A lot of people are going to be angry . . . and a lot of people are going to laugh, but it is the least a great book has to pay in a society which mesmerizes ideas into products."—*East Village Other*

"This bitter, caustic, bawdy novel rips the American establishment to pieces. . . . It is strong and imaginative, with a real shock value and a dazzling play on words."—*Publishers Weekly*

"A great writer."—James Baldwin

BY ISHMAEL REED

ESSAYS

Writin' Is Fightin'
God Made Alaska for the Indians
Shrovetide in Old New Orleans
Airing Dirty Laundry

NOVELS

Japanese by Spring
The Terrible Threes
Reckless Eyeballing
The Terrible Twos
Flight to Canada
The Last Days of Louisiana Red
Mumbo Jumbo
Yellow Back Radio Broke-Down
The Free-Lance Pallbearers

POETRY

New and Collected Poems
A Secretary to the Spirits
Chattanooga
Conjure
Catechism of D Neoamerican Hoodoo Church

PLAYS

Mother Hubbard, *formerly* Hell Hath No Fury
The Ace Boons
Savage Wilds
Hubba City

ANTHOLOGIES

The Before Columbus Foundation Fiction Anthology
The Before Columbus Foundation Poetry Anthology
Calafia
19 Necromancers from Now
Multi-America: Essays on Cultural War and Cultural Peace

THE Free-Lance Pallbearers

Ishmael Reed

Dalkey Archive Press

Library of Congress Cataloging-in-Publication Data:

Reed, Ishmael, 1938-
    The free-lance pallbearers / Ishmael Reed. — 1st Dalkey Archive ed.
    p. cm.
    ISBN 1-56478-225-5 (pa. : alk. paper)
    1. Blacks—Fiction. I. Title.
    PS3568.E365 F7 1999
    813'.54—dc21
                        99-35091
                         CIP

This publication is partially supported by grants from the Lannan Foundation, the Illinois Arts Council, a state agency, and the National Endowment for the Arts, a federal agency.

Dalkey Archive Press
Illinois State University
Campus Box 4241
Normal, IL 61790-4241

visit our website at: www.dalkeyarchive.com

Printed on permanent/durable acid-free paper and bound in the United States of America.

Dedicated to My Daughter
TIMOTHY BRETT REED

Contents

The excrement, which is what remains of all this, is loaded with our whole blood guilt. By it we know what we have murdered. It is the compressed sum of all evidence against us. It is our daily and continuing sin and as such, it stinks and cries to heaven. It is remarkable how we isolate ourselves with it. In special rooms, set aside for the purpose we get rid of it; our most private moment is when we withdraw there; we are alone only with our excrement. It is clear that we are ashamed of it. It is the age-old seal of that power-process of digestion which is enacted in darkness and which, without this, would remain hidden forever.

—Elias Canetti, *Crowds and Power*

We felt so dirty after seeing it that we felt compelled to eat at Senor Picos, a popular Mexican restaurant. We ordered the spiciest food they had just to burn ourselves out, inside.

—Shirley Temple, after seeing *Night Games*

PART I

Da Hoodoo Is Put on Bukka Doopeyduk

I live in HARRY SAM. HARRY SAM is something else. A big not-to-be-believed out-of-sight, sometimes referred to as O-BOP-SHE-BANG or KLANG-A-LANG-A-DING-DONG. SAM has not been seen since the day thirty years ago when he disappeared into the John with a weird ravaging illness.

The John is located within an immense motel which stands on Sam's Island just off HARRY SAM.

A self-made Pole and former used-car salesman, SAM's father was busted for injecting hypos into the underbellies of bantam roosters. The ol man rigged many an underground cockfight.

SAM's mother was a low-down, filthy hobo infected with hoof-and-mouth disease. A five-o'clock-shadowed junkie who died of diphtheria and an overdose of phenobarb. Laid out dead in an abandoned alley in thirty-degree-below snow. An evil lean snake with blue, blue lips and white tonsils. Dead as a doornail she died, mean and hard; cussing out her connection until the last yellow flame wisped from her wretched mouth.

But SAM's mother taught him everything he knows.

"Looka heah, SAM," his mother said before they lifted her into the basket and pulled the sheet over her empty pupils. "It's a cruel, cruel world and you gots to be swift. Your father is a big fat stupid kabalsa who is doin' one to five in Sing Sing for foolin' around with them blasted chickens. That is definitely not what's happening. If it hadn't been for those little pills, I would have gone out of my rat mind a long time ago. I have paid a lot of dues, son, and now I'm gonna pop off. But before I croak, I want to give you a little advice.

"Always be at the top of the heap. If you can't whup um with your fists, keek um. If you can't keek um, butt um. If you can't butt um, bite um and if you can't bite um, then gum the mothafukas to death. And one more thing, son," this purple-tongued gypsy said, taking a last swig of sterno and wiping her lips with a ragged sleeve. "Think twice before you speak 'cause the grave-yard is full of peoples what talks too much."

SAM never forgot the advice of this woman whose face looked like five miles of unpaved road. He became top dog in the Harry Sam Motel and master of HIMSELF which he sees through binoculars each day across the bay. Visitors to his sprawling motel whisper of long twisting corridors and passageways descending to the very bowels of the earth.

High-pitched screams and cries going up-tempo are heard in the night. Going on until the wee wee hours of the morning when everything is OUT-OF-SIGHT. Going on until dirty-oranged dawn when the bootlegged roosters crow. Helicopters spin above the motel like clattering bugs as they inspect the constant stream of limousines moving to and fro, moving on up to the top of the mountain and discharging judges, generals, the Chiefs of Screws, and Nazarene Bishops. (The Nazarene Bishops are a bunch of drop-dead egalitarians crying into their billfolds, "We must love one another or die.")

These luminaries are followed by muscle-bound and swaggering attendants carrying hand-shaped bottles of colognes, mouthwash and enema solutions—hooded men with slits for eyes moving their shoulders in a seesaw fashion as they carry trays and towels and boxes of pink tissues—evil-smelling bodyguards who stagger and sway behind the celebrated waddle of penguins in their evening clothes.

At the foot of this anfractuous path which leads to the summit of Sam's Island lies the incredible Black Bay. Couched in the embankment are four statues of RUTHERFORD BIRCHARD HAYES. White papers, busted microphones and other wastes leak from the lips of this bearded bedrock and end up in the bay fouling it so that no swimmer has ever emerged from its waters alive. Beneath the surface of this dreadful pool is a subterranean side show replete with freakish fish, clutchy and extrasensory plants. (And believe you me, dem plants is hongry. Eat anything dey kin wrap dey stems around!!)

On the banks of HARRY SAM is a park. There the old men ball their fists and say paradoxes. They blow their noses with flags and kiss dead newsreels. Legend has it that when the fateful swimmer makes it from Sam's Island to HARRY SAM, these same old men will sneeze, swoop up their skiffles and rickety sticks, then lickety-split to rooms of widow executioners in black sneakers. It is at this time that the Free-Lance Pallbearers will take SAM.

I stood outside my dean's office at the Harry Sam College. I had flunked just about everything and had decided to call it quits and marry a chick I'd been shackin' up with for a few years. I would provide for her from earnings received from working at a hospital as an orderly and where I had been promoted frequently. ("Make-um-shit Doopeyduk," the admiring orderlies had nicknamed me.) U2 Polyglot, the dean, had been very nice to me so that I couldn't conceive of leaving the hallowed halls of Harry Sam without saying good-bye to him. Just as I opened the door to his office, a sharp object struck me in dead center of the forehead. It was a paper airplane which received its doom at the tip of my toes.

"O, forgive me," U2 said. "Are you hurt? Have a Bromo Seltzer," the dumpy redheaded man in clumsy tweeds and thick glasses fizzed.

"It's all right, U2 Polyglot. I just stopped by to tell you that I was leaving school."

"Leaving school? Why how can that be, Bukka?" (My name is Bukka Doopeyduk.) "You're one of the best Nazarene apprentices here. Why, you're on your way to becoming the first bacteriological warfare expert of the colored race."

"I know that and I appreciate everything you've done for me but I am flunking just about everything and plus I'm kinda restless. I want to get married and see what's out in the world. Got to go, Polyglot."

"Well, on the other hand, maybe dropping out and tuning in will turn you on, Bukka. Who knows? But whatever you decide, I wish you a lot of luck and I'm sure that we'll be running into each other from time to time."

U2 and I shook hands and I left him to a paper he was preparing for an English literary quarterly, entitled: "The Egyptian Dung Beetle in Kafka's 'Metamorphosis.'" He had dropped to his knees and begun to push a light ball of excrement about the room by the tip of his nose. He wanted to add an element of experience to his paper. You know, give it a little zip.

That night I called Fannie Mae's home to find out if she had made the final preparations for the wedding which would take place in the parish office of Rev. Eclair Porkchop, head of the Church of the Holy Mouth. A shrill tales-of-the-crypt voice answered the phone.

"May I speak to Fannie Mae?"

"She not home."

"What time will she be in?"

"No tellin' what time she be in. Is dis you, Bukka Doopeyduk, the boy what's gone marry my granchile?"

"That's me."

"Well, I don't have to tell you how fast dese youngins is today. She probably out whipping dope needles into her mouf or somethin' lak dat."

"When she returns, would you tell her that the wedding ceremony will take place tomorrow afternoon and shortly before I must present my application to the Harry Sam Housing Projects and—"

"Hold on, Dippydick. Dis ain't no IBM factory. I'm scribbling with a chewed-up pencil and considering the fact dat I'm a spindly ol woman with two bricks for breasts, it's awful admirable dat I'm even able to take my conjur lessons through the mail under the Mojo Retraining Act. So take it from the top and go real slow." I repeated the instructions.

"Okay. I'll tell her Daffydink Dankeydim Doopeydank . . ."

"Doopeyduk."

"Whatever your name is, listen here. If you don't take good care of my granchile, I'm gonna put da hoodoo on you, and another thing . . ."

"What's that, ma'm?"

"Don't choo evah be callin' here at twelve o'clock when I'm puttin' da wolfbane on da do."

(CLICK!) She shut the phone down so hard my ears were seared. Well, that's show biz, Bukka Doopeyduk, I sighed, cakewalking my way back to the limbo of a furnished room.

We Would Need a Bigger Place

I picked up the booklet from the table in the housing project office. Above the table hung an oil portrait of SAM in a characteristic pose: zipping up the fly of butterfly-embroidered B.V.D.'s and wiping chili pepper sauce from his lips.

Next to the painting hung some employment ads:

"Passive sleep-in maid wanted."

"Apple-pickers 50¢ an hour. Must like discipline."

The cover of the booklet showed the housing manager holding the keys to an apartment. Color them gold. He smiles as he points to the Harry Sam Projects with the pose of an angel showing some looneybeard the paradise. On the next page, the typical family scene. Dad reading the papers, pipe in mouth. The little child seated on the floor busily derailing choo-choo trains, while with goo-goo eyes and smiles shaped like half-moons, the appliances operate these five rooms of enveloping bliss. And after a long list of regulations a picture of the park area. All the little children having a ball. Fountains, baby carriages and waxen men tipping their hats to waxen women.

I sat in the section where the applicants were biding their time until a woman with a sweater draped over her shoulders called their names. They were interviewed by a roly-poly man in 90 per cent rayon Sears and Roebuck pants, mod tie and nineteen-cent ball-point pen sticking from the pocket of his short-sleeve shirt, and hush puppy shoes. (No shit. Da kat must have been pushing forty and he wore hush puppy shoes and a polka-dot mod tie. Why da man looked ridiculous!)

Some of the women had electronic devices plugged into their ears. They listened to the hunchbacked housewives phone in their hernias to the bugged benzedrined eyes who negotiated toy talk for a living.

Typical: "Hello Frank? Dis Frank? Been trying to get ya ever since you come on da air. Geez kids, it's Frank. Come and say hello to ya Uncle Frank. Hiya Frank. We sure like to hear toy talk out here in Queens and Brooklyn, which brings me to the point about what I wrung ya up. You see we tink dey got too much already, running around in da streets like monkies. Why can't dey behave demselves like da res of us 'mericans. And as far as bussing wit um goes—we don't tink it'ul 'mount to much for da very simple reason dat we don't tink it's too good. Dey should help demselves like we did

when we come over on da manure dumps. Take my ol
man for an instant. Worked hisself up and now he is a
Screw. Killed fourteen hoods last week what was comin'
at um wit a knife. And my son jess shipped overseas to
put down dem Yam riots what's gettin' ready to break
loose. As you can see we are all doin' our part. Why
can't *dey?*"

But occasionally this informative chitchat would be
interrupted by a bulletin from radio UH-O:

UH-OOOOOOOOOOOOOOOOOOOOOOOOOOOOOOOOOOO
DEM CHINAMENS DONE GALLOPED INTO THE SUBURBS ON
WEREWOLF SANDALS/KIDNAPING HEEL-KICKING HOUSEWIVES
HANGING OUT DA WASH/BREAKING TV ANTENNAS OVER DERE
KNEES DEY WAYLAID COMMUTER TRAINS AND SMASHED
INK INTO THE FACES OF THE RIDERS WHO DOVE
INTO THE HUDSON TRYING TO ESCAPE/

TONS OF CREDIT CARDS SALVAGED/BULLETPROOF RICK-
SHAWS SPOTTED IN NEW ROCHELLE/(AND SOME SINISTER-
LOOKING JUNKS DONE SNEAKED INTO DA EAST RIVER TOO!)
MAJOR CRISIS SHAPING UP/SAM TO DRESS HIMSELF AS SOON
AS MAKEUP MAN ARRIVES AND THE URINALS ARE SCRUBBED.

Conorad: YAWL BETTER RUN!

"Bukka Doopeyduk," the social worker announced
through his Rudy Vallee megaphone. Sitting down he
officiously pinched his hooked nose.

On the desk were two round faces. One larger than the
other. Smiling. Wife and girl child. In a box a row of
half-chewed maraschino cherries resting in their wrappers. Gold trimmings on a get-well card which read:
"We all miss you in unit X"—followed by a list of stingy
signatures. The Nazarene priest lifted his chubby face

from the sheaf of papers he held in his hands. Rubbing
his palms together he talked.

"Sorry I kept you waitin' so long, chum, but me and
da missus were up late last night. Caught dat Sammy
out at Forest Hills. Boy dat Sammy sure can blow the
licoric stick and tickle da ivory. He was better 'n da time
we caught him at da Eleanor Roosevelt birthday cele-
bration. He was twirling his cane and kicking up wit da
spats when suddenly a miracle happened. A helicopter
landed right on da stage and out came da savior and
hope of da world. He put his arm around Sammy and
said, 'Sammy is my ace boon koon so you guys treatum
real good. Unnerstand?' Well, after dat somethin' happened dat'll just get you in da girth, I mean gird you in
da pith, I mean dere was a dearth of boos and nothin'
but stormy applause after an especially pithy ditty SAM
done about how hard it was when he was back in rat
pack p.s. Why pennies run outta da sky. You shoulda
seenum. And den da dook come on. Dat dook. His band
raised da roof beams off da joint."

"If you don't mind, your honor," I said, "I'm getting
married this afternoon so if it's all right with you, I'd
like to get on with the interview."

"Gettin' married! How wondaful. Here, have a piece
of candy," he said, pressing the chocolate into my hand.

"I don't know what to say, sir. Gee, not only are you
Nazarene priests in the Civil Service kind, but the candy
melts in your mouth and not on your hands."

"Tink nothin' of it dere, Doopeyduk. Your name is
Doopeyduk, ain't it? Where dat name come from, kiddo,
da Bible or somethin'?"

"No, sir. It came from a second cousin of my mother

who did time for strangling a social worker with custom-
made voodoo gloves."

"I see. What do you do for a living, Mr. Doopeyduk?"

"I am a psychiatric technician."

"What precisely does that involve?"

"I empty utensils and move some of our senior citizens
into a room where prongs are attached to their heads
and they bounce up and down on a cart and giggle."

"That must be engaging work."

"Yes, it is. I'm learning about the relationship between
the texture and color of feces and certain organic and/or
psychological disturbances."

"Excellent! What do you intend to do in the future?"

"Well, my work has come along so well that I have
been assigned to the preparatory surgery division of the
hospital."

"What does that involve?"

"You see, when someone undergoes a hemorrhoidec-
tomy, it's necessary that there are no hairs in the way.
I'm sort of like a barber."

"Why do you want an apartment in the Harry Sam
Projects?"

"I'm getting married this afternoon and as a Nazarene
apprentice, it behooves me to start at the bottom and
work my way up the ladder. Temperance, frugality,
thrift—that kind of thing."

"Why Mr. Doopeyduk," the priest exclaimed, removing his glasses. "I find that to be commendable! I didn't
know that there were members of the faith among your
people."

"There are millions, simply millions who wear the
great commode buttons and believe in the teachings of

Nancy Spellman, Chief Nazarene Bishop. Why, I wanted to become the first bacteriological warfare expert of the race. That was when my level of performance was lower than my level of aspiration. Now I'm just content to settle here on the home front. Wheel some of our senior citizens around, clean out the ear trumpets and empty the colostomy bags."

"The more I hear about you, the more impressed I am. You must come out and address my Kiwanis Club some-time, Doopeyduk. If there were more Negroes like you with tenacity, steadfastness, and stick-to-itiveness, there would be less of those tremors like the ones last summer, shaking SAM as if he had the palsy."

He gave me the keys to my apartment in the Harry Sam Projects and brought down the stamp of approval on my application.

That afternoon we sat in the front row of the Church of the Holy Mouth, a big Byzantine monstrosity that stood smack in the middle of Soulsville. Fannie Mae quietly chatted with her friend Georgia Nosetrouble. The two were inseparable so it seemed only natural that Georgia would be recruited as a witness.

We were waiting for Elijah Raven, a friend of mine who had consented to be best man, and of course Rev. Eclair Porkchop whose star was rising fast in SAM. Elijah was the first to arrive. He wore a dark conservative pin-striped suit and colorful beaded hat. He was bearded.

"Flim Flam Alakazam! Brothers and sisters."

Wrinkling their noses at each other, Fannie Mae and Georgia smirked.

"Flim Flam what?" I asked Elijah.

"O, of course, you wouldn't know, would you? I mean —being the brainwashed Negro you are who believes in everything that SAM runs down. Your mind is probably in the attic with all the other dummies and hand-me-downs."

"But Elijah!" I persisted. "It was only a few weeks ago that you were saying familiar things like 'Hello' or 'Hya doin'' or 'What's happening, my man.' Sometimes even slapping the palm of your hand into mine."

"That was last week. I have rejuvenated myself by joining the Jackal-headed Front. We are going to expose SAM, remove some of these blond wigs from off our women's heads, and bring back rukus juice and chittlins. You'd better get on the right side, brother, because when the deal goes down, all the backsliding Uncle Toms are going to be mowed down. You hear? Every freakin', punkish Remus will get it in the neck, Doopeyduk."

Elijah scowled, moving his finger across his neck to stress the point and revealing cuff links the size of Brazil nuts on which were engraved: "To Elijah from Sargent Shriver." But before he could expound his separatist views, the door in the back of the church opened with a slow, labored creak. I felt a chill on my shoulders and the others indicated that they too were cold.

"Ain't dey got no kindlin' in dis place?" inquired Georgia Nosetrouble.

We fixed our attention upon the door. An outline hesitated in its well. A man wearing a cape and tall hat. Removing his gloves, he seemed to float down the aisle. Soon Rev. Eclair Porkchop stood before us, resplendent in tuxedo and walking cane. Clicking his heels together, he kissed Georgia and Fannie Mae's hands.

"Good eve-a-ning. Allow me to introduce myself. I am Eclair Porkchop, head of the Church of the Holy Mouth. I am sorry to detain you but I had to do some work downtown for SAM."

"I bet that ain't all you did, you faggot and enemy of the people. When the shit hits the fan, your life ain't gone be worth two cents."

Eclair Porkchop sneered at Elijah Raven. "O, if it isn't that silly little separatist! I thought you'd be wearing a bone through your nose by now. All of that talk about going back to Africa. What happened? They dispossess your stepladder and five-dollar public-speaking permit?"

"Now see here, cocksucker," Elijah said, moving closer to the preacher.

"Break it up. Break it up. Are Fannie Mae and I going to get married or are you two going to debate?"

I looked around for Fannie Mae and Georgia who had been seated in the pews. They were nowhere to be seen. Voices came from the direction of the outer hall.

"Excuse me, gentlemen, I'll get Fannie Mae and her friend so that we can begin."

Fannie Mae and Georgia were embracing in the shadows outside the door. Georgia was sobbing. "Oh baby, what will I do without you," she panted as she massaged Fannie Mae's thighs. Seeing me, Fannie Mae removed herself from Georgia's clutch.

"What you doin', spying on us or somethin'! Can't people be by demselves sometime without you snoopin' around!!!"

"O forgive me, dearest. I didn't mean to interrupt your departure from a lifelong friend and companion," I apologized sheepishly. "But Eclair Porkchop said he had to attend a meeting over there in the motel and I thought we'd better get on with the ceremony."

"Well, yawl jess have to wait a minute."

"Of course, dear. Certainly. No rush."

The wedding ceremony was performed in the pastor's study. Afterward I bade Elijah good-bye and accepted his and Eclair Porkchop's congratulations. Georgia sadly straggled off to her home.

"Why were you and Georgia giggling at Eclair Porkchop and Elijah Raven?" I asked my new bride as we walked down the steps of the Church of the Holy Mouth.

"Both da niggahs crazy," came her reply.

"Why do you say that, dearest poppy-stick and honey-pie sugar-bunch?"

"Well, to tell it like t-i-s, Porkchop got bubble gum in his brain. Wads and wads of it hunchin' all up ginst his skull walls. I 'member when he was runnin' da numbers and selling reefers to people. Now he goin' round heah talkin' all proper, tellin' folks he been called. Hee, hee, hee. Fool sound lak Count Dracula or some spook lak dat. And dat otha niggah talkin' 'bout he don't eat pork no mo. Shoot! Me and Georgia saw him back of da Soulfood Restaurant last night. And da niggah was wearing shades so nobody'd recognize him. Next thing we know he was rolling all 'round da floor with a big hog maw 'bout to choke him to death. Dey had to call da ambulance to get some oxygen, for da fool who by then was turnin' green and callin' on da lawd, his mama and 'bout six or seven prophets to save him. Well, when dey revived him, dey removed his shades and everybody recognized him as Elijah. 'I thought you didn't eat pork, Elijah,' somebody asked. You know what da niggah

answered? What? Said dat he was doin' research on
some beast name megamorphesis. And, if you ask me,
da only beast in da place was dat hog maw which almost
carried da fool on way from heah."

As I walked arm in arm toward our new home with
my bride, an amazing thing occurred to me. Fannie Mae
knew the inside dope on everybody in Soulsville. My
sweet, innocent bride, who was fond of saying, "I loves
to party and I know where I can find a party," was
really together.

Fannie Mae and I stood near the amusement truck
outside the Harry Sam Projects. The rides consisted of
plastic and stainless steel drolls, giraffes and horses. The
children were chitterwhimpering and higgledy-piggledy
playing pickaback. A statue of HARRY SAM reigned
over all, this time standing with his hands draped over
two marvelous Victorian urinals. A black Screw sat at
the entrance to the high-rise building that contained our
apartment. (Screws are men armed with turkey muskets
who patrol HARRY SAM.) At his feet was a victrola
which played the jug music of a hot Memphis band.
He wore a cracked cowbell around his neck marked
Carnegie. (Elijah Raven and his gang had placed it
there telling him that it was an award in recognition of
his valor for preventing homicide by mediating a dispute
over highjacked piecrust which involved several tenants.
The bell provided an early warning system for the Jackal-
headed Front busily involved in some sinister pranks in
the Harry Sam Projects.)

He slept while flies zoomed around his bean. Like the
nasty little dive bombers they were, they dashed against
his forehead. He jerked, one eyelid open and one shut,
then went back to sleep.

Fannie Mae and I reached the door of our apartment and I put the key into the latch. Wheezing, I lifted Fannie Mae for the traditional threshold caper.

"Put me down, fool! You simple or somethin'?"

"But Fannie Mae, dearest. This is included in the marriage rite prescribed by the Nazarene manual."

"Aw dem white folks done fussed yo skull wit all dat crazy talk. Let's go inside like somebody's got some sense. You come on like some senile mailman with a case of dropsy."

Inside we examined the five empty rooms of our first apartment. Through the walls came the voices of our neighbors: "Who ate dat last piece of pie son of a bitch you ate it who ate it he ate it then what's the crust doin' in you greasy choppers if he ate it cause he snuck and ate it while you was sleepin' fool did you eat the pie yes I ate it woman you gone whup me about it aw woman don't whip da man let him res woman why don't you jess hush and let peoples res. . . ."

Outside the belching of foghorns. The interminable helicopters. The snow falling. EATS EATS EATS EATS.

The next morning my father-in-law called. A ninety-year-old punkish-looking mothball, he was devoted to thumb-sucking and living with the tales-of-the-crypt voice who decorated his house with crocheted pillows of Niagara Falls. He had been president of the colored Elks in 1928 and once kissed Calvin Coolidge's ass. He now sat about the house all day drinking Champale malt liquor and watching daytime melodramas on TV. Cobwebbed antlers rested upon his head.

He said, "Fannie Mae, dahlin'. I am spitting up dese

colors, see, and I would like for you to come over and put some pink powder in between my toes for dey is crawlin' wit what appears to be some kind of anamuls. Also, baby, as you know, I is real sceered of da dak. Dere are dese spooky shapes sitting atop my bedposts and dey won't go a-way, no matter how hard I huff and puff. Now baby, you know dat don't make no kind of sense. Yo daddy, as you will recall, was da head of da colored Elks in 1928 and I must send out correspondences. Granmama put some Uncle Jeeter's powder under da pillow and dat didn't seem to help a-tall. In fact, DEM SPECTERS DONE GOT BOLDER! Please come over and shoo dem away 'cause dey is makin' me wet the bed and scream and hollah fo Granmama who's tryin' to get her witchcraft doctorate and make somethin' out of herself. I will expect you fust ting in da morning and tings can be da way dey was 'fo you married dat boy what sticks prongs in people's heads and makes dem bounce up and down lak dey is some kinda acrobat. Dis is da Grand Exalted Ruler of da Elks signin' over to his daughter." (Click.)

"My father wants me to come over to his house and read old-timey pamphlets to him," Fannie Mae announced. "I'll be back in two weeks."

"Why can't his mother do that?"

"She's taking a course under the Mojo Power Retraining Act, dat's why. You so simple."

"Somebody ought to take a stick and bang the big sissy upside the head with it. Rusty dusty overgrown Mickey Mouse flapper afraid of the dark and calling for that ogress. Heh, heh, heh."

"Don't be thinkin' ugly 'bout my family. You're jess jealous 'cause he was da head of da colored Elks in 1928 and all you can do is take care of all dem screwballs skipping around what needs a shrink."

"Well, a kat who sits in the house all day wearing a moose headpiece got a whole lot of marbles to collect."

"Don't be laffin' at my daddy," Fannie Mae said, hurling a pan of lye at me. I ducked and the solution went through the window. Below, there was the sudden clang of a cowbell accompanied by a scream. Then many klang-a-langs in rapid succession quietly dying in the distance.

"I was just jokin', dearest. Don't get excited."

"You best be jokin'. Now I'm gone go over to Daddy's and take care of him. Dere is some week-old green chickens dat I bought at Gooseman's supermarket for seventy cents a pound. You can nibble on dat for a while." She threw her garment about her and rushed from the apartment.

But she forgot something. I went to the closet and removed a plastic container from the shelf. I opened the window and yelled at Fannie Mae.

"YOU FORGOT SOMETHIN', SWEET PICKLE BUNCH."

"Whatchawont?"

"You forgot . . . the antler polish," I screamed.

Fannie Mae escaped from her dad's house just as her grandmother was about to shove her into the oven in one of the grimmer exercises prescribed by the witchcraft syllabus. We met our neighbors shortly after she returned home. Our only contact with them had been the creaking of bedsprings and the "O sock it to me good joogie woogie" that came through the rice paper the housing authorities tried to pass off as a wall. Riding in the elevator one day, having just returned from work, I stood next to a man who was reading a comic book. He seemed amused by its cover: *King Kong atop the Empire State Building with the Joint Chiefs of Staff wriggling in one hand while the other hand is flinging down all the fuken airplanes.*

Also aboard the elevator was a Nazarene apprentice and two children. The children were involved in a scuffle.

"Gimmie my cap. Gimmie back my cap," said one to the other. One child drew back his fist and was about to strike his companion when the Nazarene apprentice put down his clipboard and intervened.

"Now children, you mustn't fight. HARRY SAM won't hold you in his lap when he comes out of the comfort station."

The children looked at one another curiously before examining the priest.

"How would HARRY SAM like this?" one of the children said, before hauling off and kicking the priest in the shins.

The other child delivered a quick karate chop whose impact caused the priest to slump to the floor in a coocoo daze. I nudged the man standing next to me.

"Don't you think that we ought to put an end to this?"

"Aw dem jess chirren playing," was his reply.

I was about to pull the children from the helpless Nazarene apprentice when the elevator opened and they scooted out between the legs of the black Screw who was walking down the hallway. The cowbell was jarred. Ting ting. Half of the Screw's face was white. The Screw unbound the Nazarene apprentice and removed the gag from his mouth as the man reading the book and I walked toward our respective apartments.

"No tellin' what dese kids gone be doin' next," the Screw philosophized.

"Thanks," said the Nazarene apprentice, assembling his scattered notes and the copy of the magazine *Studies on the Flank.*

"Here, let me hep you up suh."

"Don't bother, Screw. What on earth happened to the other side of your face, Screw?"

"I don't know, suh. I was sitting out de doors yestiddy and some fire rain come out da sky and scalded my face."

"Fire rain. Isn't that interesting? One of those many bizarre happenings in the ghettos, I presume. O, this is so thrilling! I even enjoyed the roughing up those kids gave me. You see, I'm working on a paper on the mores of segregated housing projects for the University of Chicago. I might even write this incident up in a magazine I edit called *Studies on the Flank.* It enabled me to observe culturally deprived children at first hand."

"Kulchur prived chirren? What's dat Yo Excellency?"

"O that means they can't go to Lincoln Center and devour Lilly Ponds."

"Wait a minute. Wait a minute, suh. Hold on. Now, I'm jess a poor Screw who is a traitor and abomination of my peoples but even I know dat Lilly Ponds ain't gone hep dese kids. Dey needs somethin' stantial in dey stomicks, like roast pork or steak. Lilly Ponds! Why dat's food fishes eat, ain't it?"

The flies which constantly swirled about the black Screw's head suddenly buzzed into the face of the Nazarene apprentice before he could reply. The elevator door closed as the Screw repeatedly slapped the apprentice so as to relieve him from his latest misfortune. The apprentice cooed in ecstasy.

In the hall the neighbor spoke to me. "You must be the couple that moved in here a few weeks ago."

"That's right. My name is Bukka Doopeyduk. What's yours?"

"My mother lost my name in a lottery, Mr. Doopeyduk. Why don't you jess call me the neighbor, and so's you kin 'stinguish between me and my wife, refer to me as M/Neighbor and my wife as F/Neighbor."

"Fine with me," I said. "I have a hard time remembering names anyway."

"Why don't you and your wife come over and get 'quainted tonight? Dere's plenty of rukus juice and chittlins, Bukka Doopeyduk. You lak chittlins?"

"Yes, indeed, I do," I said. "The ancient Etruscans ate them, you know."

"I don't know nothin' 'bout no truscans, but I know dey is good."

It was apparent that the intellectual diet I had become accustomed to at the Harry Sam College was remiss in the projects. But I had become bored with my Mahler records and had studied the Nazarene manual so often that the pages were dog-eared. Besides, Fannie Mae was getting restless. Maybe getting together with the neighbors might do her some good. No matter how dull they were.

"Fine. I accept your generous invitation."

"Good, Doopeyduk. You and your wife come over about seven. Okay?"

"Seven it is," I said, opening the door to my apartment.

Fannie Mae was curled up on the sofa watching the Art Linkletter show where a life supply of pigeons had been awarded to four cripples and some parents of children with harelip.

"How was it at the hospital today?"

"Nothing unusual. They bumped off a couple of old geezers whose insurance had run out, dear."

"How can you stand workin' round dem crazy people? Why don't you go out to da Harry Sam Ear Muffle Factory? Georgia Nosetrouble asked me why you hadn't. She said dat she had lost sleep tryin' to figure out why you hadn't gone out to da Harry Sam Ear Muffle Factory to see if you couldn't get a job, tossing ear muffles into a box like all da res of da mens round here. She said dat she wondered what you thought made you so special. Dey make some good change too, for dat little pipsqueak, skinny-assed check you bring home don't pay for the fun I likes to have. Da blond wigs I ordered from Mlle. Pandy Matzabald haven't been paid for yet."

"You just don't understand me, dear. I'm not the type that could withstand the steady demoralization that a routine job like that would cause. You see, as a Nazarene apprentice, I'm interested in finding out what makes people tick."

"Dey don't wash demselves. Dat's why dey tick."

"You're always poking fun at my job. Why did you consent to marry me if you didn't respect my work?"

"I wanted to get away from dat crazy woman who's my daddy's mother. She was gettin' ready to shove me into da oven allatime in preparation for her sorcery exams. Da cinders were ruining my dresses. You were da first mark to come along who wanted to remove me from dat situation. So you're boss in my book. Anyway, I like da way you talk. It's cute."

"Gee, Fannie Mae, for a moment there, you had me

worried. I didn't think there was mutual warmth and respect between us. The Nazarene manual demands that of young couples."

"See, dat's what I mean. You're sweet. You talk different."

"Guess what the doctor said today, Fannie Mae, dearest?"

"What he say?"

"Said that he thought I'd be working in the shock room soon. Said he'd never seen me shirk my responsibility so that if I didn't shuck anybody soon, I'd be in the shock room."

"He say shuck?"

"Sure, Fannie Mae. He's a real hippy. Reads *Evergreen Review* and eats cheese blintzes at *Max's Kansas City*, a place where all the artists hang out downtown. Mixes with us orderlies and is crazy about Duke Ellington. Anyway the shock room is a place we wheel people into and boom the living daylights out of their brains so that they can return to normal life and behave themselves like the rest of us 'mericans. I'll be in charge of the tongue blades. You really have to be on top of yourself to hold down a job like that."

"It better be on top of yourself and not on top of none of dem fast women dat work up dere. If I ever hear dat you are servin' as prop for some women's tongues, I'll slash your clothes."

"Aw cut it out, Fannie Mae. I put the blade on the patient's tongue. This requires considerable expertise and it also means a five-dollar raise."

"Well, I hope it hurries up and happens. I sho don't feel like sittin' round here all day when Georgia Nosetrouble and me can be in the movies watchin' some fine lookin' man like Gregory Peck and Troy Donahue. And speakin' of good-lookin' mens, why don't you get yo hair konkalined? Yo hair looks nappy. Why don't you slick it down with some lye?"

"What's the use?" I said, walking up to my ankles in the slush on the kitchen floor. When I opened the frig, *something grabbed at me*. I shut it quickly.

"Damn Fannie Mae! Why don't you clean the place out sometimes? These blobs in the frig are about to invade the kitchen."

"MOTHAFUKAAAAAAAAAAAAAA. What do you think I am, some kind of bowlegged pack animal who's gone empty your slops dat you can keek and give orders to? If you want somebody to clean dis place, why don't you get somebody to come in and do daywork." She waved her hands and screeched like the real scourge of a scrounge she was.

"Ok doky," I said meekly, as she went to the phone to dial the Screws.

"Now next time you raise your voice at me, I'm gone get da MAN downtown on you."

"I was just kiddin' honey, little mommy and sweet poppy-stick."

She returned to the television where SAM was making an announcement from the low-down nasty room.

"Slurp, slurp. Dis is the boss, folks. SAM. Slurp. Now I'm not gonna get all flowery like the fella what preceded me, quotin' all them fellas what wore laurels and nightgowns. I'm gonna give you people the straight dope. Now dere's rumors goin' round here that the Chinamens 'bout to run away wit all our fine suburban women. I know that all who loves SAM HIMSELF and ME all in one realize that your man would never tolerate no little yellow dwarfs wit pocketknives slashing our women's discothèque pants, hip boots, miniskirts or none of them otha fashions that me and Mlle. Pandy Matzabald thunk up for um to wear. Slurp, slurp.

"So that you folks won't get all alarmed, I'm gonna send ABOREAL HAIRYMAN out there to Westchester to check this stuff out. You all know A.B., a nice gent who uses big words like quibbicale, that I drug out of the Seventeen Nation Disarmament Conference gin mill and made a roving ambazzador. Now when A.B. comes back, I'll clue you in on what's happening.

"Now one more ting before I get back to the low-down nasty room where Mlle. Pandy Matzabald can go downtown on me. To the creeps on the steps of Sprool Hall at Berkeley. KEEP IT UP YOU FREE-LOADEN COMMUNISTS TAFFYPANTS SISSIES. I GOT MY EYES ON YOU AND YOUR MINISTRATORS HAVE PASSED ON YOUR NAMES TO ME. JUST KEEP IT UP AND MY SCREWS WILL CLAMP DOWN ON YOU SO HARD PUNKS DAT YOU'LL WISH THAT YOU WAS DEAD. DON'T FORGET NOTHIN' ESCAPES MY EYES SINCE I GOT THESE HERE BINOCULARS WITH THE FORTY BOOKS OF GREEN STAMPS.

"And also to the jerk who said back there a week ago that I wasn't given you 'mericans the smart money odds on the way tings was going down in ME. Yeah wise guy. I read what you had to say about my foreign matters and you know what I tink about it. It's shit. That's what it is. Shit. So get lost buddy and shaddup. What my cutie pies don't know, won't hurtum.

"Excuse me for gettin' all steamed up, little pink pussies. But when these clowns say I'm not lookin' out for ya, IT MAKES ME MAD! UNNERSTAND? Because

you know that I'm nuts about ya. Gotta go now, all you
little pimple-pie poopsies.

"This was Daddy. Take it easy, toots. Don't take no
wooden nickels and if you do, name um after me. Har,
har, har, har. Good night, good night, good night. I hate
to say good night. When the moon comes over the mountain and wherever you are Mrs. Kalabash. . . . "

(Dictators have always fumbled their exits.)

"Kee, kee, kee. Dat man tickles me."

"Fannie Mae," I said. "You're not supposed to put down
our leader like that. Why . . . why . . . I loves the man."
I fell to my knees and repeated the oaths I'd learned at
the Harry Sam College: "Harry Sam does not love us. If
he did, he'd come out of the John and hold us in his lap.
We must walk down the street with them signs in our
hands. We must throw back our heads and loosen our
collars. We must bawl until he comes out of there and
holds us like it was before the boogeyman came on the
scene and everybody went to church and we gave each
other pickle jars each day and nobody had acne nor
bad breath and cancer was just the name of a sign."

"Aw fool, get up off da damn flo. You look ridiculous."

"Fannie Mae, you're not supposed to interrupt me
when I'm repeating my vows."

"I'm not going to argue with you. I have to go downtown to Mlle. Pandy Matzabald's head shop and pick up
my wig."

"Well, when you come back, the neighbors want us to
come over and have supper with them."

"Good, den I can leave da green chickens till tomorrow."

"You'd need the Seventh Fleet to get into our frig anyway, it's so full of arrogant bacteria."

"What you say?"

"Nothin' dear. Hurry back."

The neighbor's wife greeted us. She wore a hairdo
called the porcupine quill. Her feet were chalked and
her dress was covered with sunflower prints.

"Come on in, yawl, and res you self. My husband told
me dat you was gone stop over tonight. We is all home
folks so don't be shamefacedy. M/Neighbor is 'n da
baffroom but he be out directly. De rukus juice is on da
livin'-room table and da chittlins is stirring and da hog
jile and egg pone is jes comin' long swell. Dere's some
oldie but goodie records on da victrola so yawl jes go on
in while I makes da res of da suppa." In the living room
two pictures hung side by side on the wall. One of
J/Christ and the other of Jacqueline Kennedy's riding
boots.

M/Neighbor came from the bathroom. "Why looka
heah, if it ain't Mister and Missus Doopeyduk. Glad you
could come by. Here, let me pour you some rukus juice,"
he said, filling our glasses with Thunderbird wine. We
took a drink and were further accosted by the neighbor's
solicitations. Suddenly, rapid and spirited discussion came
from a room in the rear of the apartment.

"Do other people live here?" I asked.

"Dat's my teen-ager," the neighbor replied. "He's in
da back room with a friend who visits him. Little white
boy named Joel O. Dey got maps of SAM in dere on da
wall."

"Maps of SAM? Why that's absurd," I said. "SAM's

nothing but a o-bop-she-bang-a-klang-a-lang-a-ding-dong
an out-of-sight not-to-be-believed . . ."

"Yes, that's what they always told me and you, Mr.
Doopeyduk. But dese smart-aleck kids tink dey can figure
da MAN out."

"This I have to see. Will you call them in here?"

"Sho, Doopeyduk. M/NEIGHBOR'S TEEN-AGER!"

"Whatchawont, Pop?" came the reply from the room.
"Me and Joel O. are studying for the lecture tonight
down at the B.B.B. Club."

"Boy, when I tell you to do something, you do it, boy.
Understand, boy? Now git yo tail in here and talk to us
grown peoples. Pay attention to what grown peoples be
saying."

"But grown people don't say anything of significance
any more, Pop. They're just a bunch of middle-aged
rukus-juice drinkers who drop bombs on people and
listen to that smelly man who's been holed up in the
John for thirty years."

I was appalled. "What! WHAT THE CHILD SAY?"

But before I could register my shock, the neighbor
had slapped his son's face.

"What did you have to go and do that for, Pop?"
he asked, as the little white boy comforted him.

"Listen heah," M/Neighbor continued, rukus juice
hanging from his lips in spidery strings. "Repeat after me.
In my father's house . . ."

"In my father's house . . ."

"What grown peoples be saying . . ."

"But Pop. That's not even correct grammar."

"Damn the grammar, you black-assed bastard. Now
repeat after me before I smacks you again. What grown
peoples be saying . . ."

"What grown peoples be saying . . ."

"Is not never supposed to be joked around about."

"Is not never supposed to be joked around about," the M/Neighbor's son replied. "Now, can me and Joel O. go down to the B.B.B. meeting?" he asked. Joel stood next to him wearing a parka. His hair was draped about his shoulders and on his chest he wore a "Flower-Power" button.

"Where you mannish kids going tonight? Don't be comin' in heah all time of da night again no mo. Dat boy Joel O. has got his own apartment and he can do what he wants to do but yo tail has to answer to me 'cause I'm footin' the bills . . . And before you go, 'pologize to Mr. Doopeyduk for getting him all upset."

"I'm sorry, Mr. Doopeyduk."

"That's all right, my boy. But you must always be careful about what you say about our great leader. You only give aid and comfort to our enemies when you speak ill of him. Of course you kids were only speaking in jest."

"Jest, hell," the little white boy said for the first time. "When we come to power, it's going to be curtains for the generation that gave us Richard Nixon and his scroungy mutt, Checkers."

"See you later, Pop, and it was a pleasure meeting you, Mr. and Mrs. Doopeyduk."

"Ciao," said the little white boy as the pair walked out of the door.

"Why, I must lodge a protest tomorrow morning about this man who's subverting the young youth. Report this subversive to the authorities. How long has this been going on, M/Neighbor?"

"Dey always be readin' some kinda books. Got da

author's picture on da wall. He's a colored man but he look lak one of dem Anglishmens. Wears a goatee. Sometime dey wear dem tablecloths what African peoples wear and dat little white boy be talkin' funny. Two, three words at a time. Somethin' 'bout 'psychedelic guerrilla/ Mao Mao/ folkrock fuckrock Ra cock/ freak stomp group grope/ sunra's marimbas/ yin yang.' It's way over my poor brains. And da B.B.B. thing supposed to stand for SAM has got body odor."

"That does it," I said, rushing to the telephone to dial the Screws.

"Aw fool, set yo butt down. Dem boys jess tryin' to have some fun," Fannie Mae said, after remaining silent throughout the entire episode.

F/Neighbor walked into the room with the platter of steaming hot chittlins and a side dish of potato salad.

"A man what's been in the baffroom fo thirty years— no tellin' what he smell like," Fannie Mae continued.

"I gots to go along wif you, child," the F/Neighbor interjected. "Unless he got a powerful deodorant, he smellin' like dese chittlins when dey's cookin'. But less stop talkin' 'bout polotics and eats some food. Dere's plenty."

Although shocked at these pronouncements, the neighbor and I were so taken by the meal that we decided not to pursue the matter.

After the dinner, I asked, "Do you have any more children?"

F/Neighbor rose from the table and ran sobbing into the living room. Fannie Mae went after to comfort her.

UH O, I thought. You've made a blimp of a blooper this time, Bukka Doopeyduk.

The M/Neighbor explained. "We had a child dat disappeared around three years ago."

"Didn't you have the Screws look into the matter?"

"Yes, dey searched. But dey couldn't find hide nor hair of him."

The women returned. F/Neighbor, red-eyed and stunned. Fannie Mae assisted her into the chair.

"I'm sorry, F/Neighbor. I wasn't aware of your loss," I said.

"Dat's all right, Mr. Doopeyduk. I should have gotten over it by now. By the way, Mr. Doopeyduk," F/Neighbor asked, "does that name come out da Bible?"

"No, my mother won it in a lottery."

They all laughed and I was pleased that my quip had helped to glide over an unpleasant and embarrassing incident. Afterward we played whist. I couldn't get the missing child out of my mind. I looked out over the M/Neighbor's shoulder toward the island across the bay. The helicopters dipped and rose above the roof. Again the snow. The stillness. The four letters, EATS.

I came home one day, walking dejectedly, grumbling. I had been demoted from the shock room. I had placed a tongue blade into a banker's mouth carelessly and he had nearly strangled to death. He was a powerful and influential man in HARRY SAM who had been picked up by the Screws for enticing sailors and was placed on the psychiatric floor to avoid publicity. His psychiatrist had witnessed the mishap and had reprimanded me before the nurses. They cut my salary and placed me in a ward with the violent patients. My job was to clean the wastes which hung from the walls in gobs and change the catatonic patients. I was in a miserable mood when I arrived at the apartment.

Fannie Mae was entertaining Georgia who sat in a chair smoking a cigarette butt and swinging her legs. When she saw me, she nodded disinterestedly and continued smacking her gum.

"Georgia and her husband are goin' to move into da projects building next to ours," Fannie Mae announced.

I nodded at the girl, who smiled mischievously, then picked up a comic book lying on the coffee table. I stepped over the comic books which were strewn about the house and walked into the bathroom. The house was filthy. The dishes filled the sink, clogging it so that I expected some pulsating thing to reach out and assimilate me into the decayed eggs, meat and vegetables. The place stank of food. The refrigerator contained provisions crawling with bacteria.

"Dear," I said, "why don't you at least try to keep the house in a sanitary condition?" I pleaded. "It looks like a pigsty."

"Don't start no mess," she replied, looking at Georgia for support.

Blood rushed to my head. I gritted my teeth and threw a glass against the wall. The women ignored this, continuing to read the books and chatting with each other.

"Why don't you get up off your big funkey sometime and pick up a mop? I break my ass emptying shit at the hospital and you lay around here all day, half-dressed, watching 'The Edge of Night,' 'Search for Tomorrow' and 'The Guiding Light.'"

"Look, my man. Nobody told you to get that job. At

the Harry Sam Ear Muffle Factory they makes good money."

"Why don't you get a job and help me, tramp? Plenty of women work nowadays. What's so special about you? 'Round here lying on the floor reading comic books like some empty half-wit."

The picture of Nancy Spellman dressed like a little red Kewpie doll swung around on the wall and crashed to the floor below. Nancy was the Chief Nazarene Bishop. Poor Nancy, I thought.

"See what you made me do, bitch! Nancy Spellman fell off the wall."

"I'm sick of dem sweetback-looking white mens on my wall anyway."

Georgia Nosetrouble snickered behind the comic book.

Fannie Mae got up from the sofa, and hands on hips, feet spread apart, spoke hot fire.

"DERE'S PLENTY OF KONKALINED PORKPIE BEANIES 'ROUND HERE WHO THINK I LOOK VEWY VEWY GREAT. YOU START SOME MESS AND I'LL SLASH YOUR CLOTHES AND THROW THE FURNITURE OUT OF THE WINDOW. What's wrong wit dese mens today, Georgia?"

"Don't ask me, Fannie Mae. Must be some bug going around."

"What you got to do with it, Georgia? What are you doing moving in here anyway? You jamming this ho."

Rising to get her wrap, Georgia pouted, squinted her eyes and threatened me.

"Looka heah, Doopeyduk, whatever yo name is. I am not yo wife. Fuk with me and I'll really give you something to complain about."

Nancy's portrait was damaged beyond recognition. All
that remained were the puckered lips, the twinkly eyes.
Fannie Mae lurched for the door.

"Don't go, Georgia. He jess showin' out fo company."
She followed the girl into the hall. When she came back
into the apartment, she laced into me.

"Now I guess you satisfied. She wasn't botherin' you,
but you had to show yo ass. Dippyduk goofy mother-
grabber!" And then grumbling, she went hissing into the
bedroom, slamming drawers and after an hour in the
bathroom profuse with whucking faucets and the opening and shutting of cabinets, she came out heavily made
up. She whisked past me and stalked into the hall tapping
her foot impatiently as she waited for the elevator to
come up.

"What time do you intend to come back?" I asked
submissively.

"Nighttime! And if you try to follow me, I'll get a jeep
full of dem Screws with turkey muskets after you."

I went all out. Through my whole crying-the-blues
repertory, even pulling a few new tricks out of the hat.
Like—

"Fannie Mae, Fannie Mae, please don't go, sugar,
'cause iffin you leave me, I'll have bread done on one
side, 'cause the toaster broke down, I'll cry a fistful of
clock hands over you, and walk the third rail, boo hoo
boo hoo. What I gonna do? Consult the hoodoo man.
Woe is me."

But my words slap-dashed against the elevator door
and slid down to the floor. My baby had done gone.
The little children who had given the Nazarene apprentice the hassle were standing next to the elevator door.
I stood there in my orderly uniform with the black stripe

down the side of the pants. The kids broke up, rolling about the floor and laughing.

I went back inside and saw that my fly had been open during the entire episode. Embarrassed, I walked to the window just as the moon peeped over the summit of Sam's Island. Fannie Mae and Georgia were hightailing it toward the lights from the jooks which surrounded the projects. I drunk some likker and got my head bad. At three o'clock in the morning there came a tap-dap-rapping at my door. A tit-tat-klooking at my hollow door.

"Who is dat rap-a-dap-tapping at my do' this time of night? What-cha wont?"

"Have you seen some children playing in this vicinity?" asked the lean woman dressed in black. She shivered, clutching the top of her housecoat.

"No, I haven't," I lied, hoping that they'd been swallowed by the incinerator or some equally grisly fate had befallen them.

Mr. and Mrs. Nosetrouble moved into the projects shortly after that night. At last the Harry Sam Projects were integrated. Mr. Nosetrouble was white and the statue of HARRY SAM winked slyly from one stony eye. The moving van pulled up and dumped the basket chairs, bound and musty pamphlets, fish tanks, flags, short-wave radios, plants, chickadees, espresso machines, Band-Aids. Tumbling out behind these were stacks upon stacks of foreign language newspapers, and a fine little case. When the men started to throw this black leather case upon the rest of the items, Georgia's husband had a fit.

"Wait a minute, wait a minute. Where you goin' wit that case? Have a little respect, fellas. The nose inside

that case belong to none other than L. Trotsky who in
a speech before the cemetery at Prague said 'Blimp Blank
Palooka Dookey,' and standing in a threadbare coat,
shaking his fist in the rain for hours, said 'Blank Palooka
Dookey Blimp' and who on more than one occasion
warned the ruling circles 'Dookey Palooka Blank Blimp.'"

The two husky movers scratched their heads and
grinned at little Nosetrouble as he scampered into the
building, precious black case in hand. Nosetrouble was
Crazzzzzzzzzzzzzzzzy about the workers. Wanted to be
around them all the time and wear the workers' clothes
and eat the workers' food and drink the workers' drink
and look at um all a time. Once Nosetrouble raised such
a stink in HARRY SAM that SAM had to go into a huddle
with his washroom attendants. But being the sellout hippies that they were, they came up with a slick ploy.

SAM went on television. Sitting at a workman's bench
he patted a little cocker spaniel on the head. They had
applied synthetic soot to his face. He took a swig of beer
from a can and addressed the nation.

"Hi folks. The MAN here again. Got a few minutes
before the whistle is blown on us down in the John, a
signal for me to go back to work. Didn't know I worked,
did you dumplings? Pardon me. . . ." (He took a sand-
wich from a brown bag and filled his mouth to the
brink of his lips with liverwurst.)

"At least all those who know me and love me 'preciates
the fact that I work, which makes it come as a surprise
when these people go around here bitchin' about the
way I handle the workers.

"Geeze, folks, solidarity forever and o yeah while I'm
at it, we shall overcome. Hell, I got injured in an industrial accident once, see?" The dictator raised his

nightshirt and pointed to a scar which traveled north from the spine to his left breast.

The *New York Times* called the speech an eloquent and poignant plea for industrial peace.

Georgia's husband was mauled the next day by the workers for being a tool of jabberwocky conspirators who's ginst us 'mericans. He was nearly lynched when they discovered the two slices of Polish ham in his lunch pail.

"We ain't innerstead in L. Trotsky's nose," the workers said in chorus as they gave Nosetrouble the old heave-ho. They began to chant in fact: "TOY TALK/ TOY TALK/ WE WANT TOY TALK/ TOY TALK/ TOY TALK/ WE WANT TOY TALK/ JING-A-LING/ DIPSY NOODLE/ N.B.C. and/ COCK-A-DOODLE/ TOY TALK/ TOY TALK/ WE WANT/ TOY TALK."

Nosetrouble never forgot the humiliation. He moved into the Harry Sam Projects and vowed to get the tenants involved in direct action. He received no help from the other labor leaders. Indeed, they were the most avid visitors to the dark and gloomy motel which loomed over not-to-be-believed. Why, women would jump out of cakes for them. Little boys would entertain them with madrigals. Each night they carried their toilet articles in eerie procession like the judges, generals, and Chief of Screws who had preceded them. They were second only to the leaders of the blacks who mounted the circuitous steps leading to SAM's, assuring the boss dat: "Wasn't us, boss. 'Twas Stokely and Malcolm. Not us, boss. No indeed. We put dat ad in da *Times* repudiating dem, boss. 'Member, boss? You saw da ad, didn't you, boss? Look, boss. We can prove it to you, dat we loves you. Would you like for us to cook up some strange recipes

for ya, boss? Or tell some jokes? Did you hear the one
about da nigger in da woodpile? Well, seems dere was
this nigger, boss . . ."

SAM would sit stone-faced under this steady barrage
of limericks, slapstick and handstands and hoedowns
and jigs and cotillions until he'd finally melt.

"Har, har, har. You boys sure know the Bible good."

Georgia's husband had also been abandoned by the
others who carried around L. Trotsky's hair in their pock-
etbooks inbetween the diaphragms. They had moved
into quaint little towns in the thicket of SAM called
Freedom Village. They itched SAM once in a while by
showing up on picket lines with their teased hair and
Montgomery Ward originals, holding aloft signs which
read: "For Heaven Sakes Allready, Don't Bomb Our
Swimming Pools." Or they took ads in the *Times* which
read: "We the undersigned are unalterably opposed to
misery." Followed by five hundred handsome names.

But despite his idiosyncrasies, Nosetrouble was an in-
trepid and scrappy little guy. As soon as he settled in the
projects, his campaign began. He accused the soap companies of not putting enough powder into the tubs of
dead laundromats. And that if it wasn't put in by two
weeks, he and his committee would put the whammy on
high-strung police horses, causing them to throw their
riders.

The soap companies gave in, sending out a statement:
"How was we supposed to know? Are there washroom
signs in our brains? A dozen boxes of Oxydol will be
sent over first ting inda morning. Tanks for being innerstead in the tubercular tubs. All spots will be removed
from their revolving lungs." The souls were confused by
the issue.

But next washday when the clothes came out sparkling white, the housewives lifted Nosetrouble to their shoulders and paraded him through the projects. Victory! Now Georgia's husband would consolidate his gains and move for a showdown with the low-down occupant of the bottoms himself. Nosetrouble was getting the goods on the self-made Pole and former Plymouth pusher.

Fannie Mae had left earlier in the day. I had given her money for groceries and she decided to look in on the Nosetroubles, now in the middle of unpacking. I remained indoors to nurse some lumps received the night before while coaxing a patient into the room which contained the little black box. My general appearance had deteriorated. I was beginning to look fierce. Ill-tempered and morose, I flew off the handle at the slightest provocation. My hair had grown long and shaggy and stubby patches began to appear on my face. I no longer carried myself in the proud erect style of the Nazarene apprentices, but shambled along with my shoulders drooped and my chin pinned to my neck. I slept a lot and would arrive late for work under the hawk eye of a piqued head nurse. Increasingly, I would go to M/Neighbor's apartment and get stoned. We would drink until the stuff trickled down the corners of our mouths.

That afternoon, while watching a succession of kiddie shows, F/Neighbor came into the room where her husband and I sat.

"Mr. Doopeyduk. Now I don't want to get into yo business but seems lak someone done put the hoodoo on you. Why don't you go out and buy some John the Conquerer roots?"

"Why that's absurd," I said. "It's just a bug. That's all. It'll go away."

"Don't look lak no bug to me. I never seen nobody bugged dat had fangs and pointed ears. No, I think dat you have definitely been hoodooed."

"You superstitious lame-brain! I don't know why I've been wasting all this time with your type of backward riffraff anyway. Why, I could be listening to some interesting Nazarene lecture on radio station WBAI."

I stalked from the room and slammed their door behind me. Inside the apartment, I dozed off and dreamed:

I am walking through a forest of eucalyptus trees. Sunbeams like millions of fireflies show through the foliage. A hooded woman guides me to a clear mountain lake. Vegetation can be seen at its shallow bottom. She removes her shoes and wades through the lake to a cliff which borders one side. Below the cliff, the thunderous sound of a primeval ocean. She beckons me to follow her, hinting that there are wondrous sights below. In the distance, there are mountains smoldering from dormant volcanoes. As I step into the lake, dark tentacles rush me. I escape, climbing back upon the bank now packed with fancy objects (associated wit what peoples in da West call BA-ROKE or somethin' lak dat). She lowers her hood and laughs. Suddenly Nancy Spellman appears on the bank. He is dressed in his little red smock and red skull cap. He chastises the woman who flees into the forest. He holds a sign which reads: EAT AT SAM'S. THREE TRIPS PER DAY.

My shirt clung to my body. The area about my genitals was damp. I went into the hall without bothering to groom myself. People were surrounding the woman who had knocked on my door in search of the missing children.

"Dey gone, dey gone," she was saying. "Dey jess vanished in thin air."

I scowled at the gathering and rushed past the amusement truck toward the apartment of Mr. and Mrs. Nosetrouble. Nosetrouble answered the door.

"Have you seen Fannie Mae?"

"They went outta here 'bout three hours ago. Said they were going to a movie. Why don't you come on in and wait, Mr. Doopeyduk? You can be one of the first to be in on my grand strategy for gettin' the goods on SAM."

He was having trouble with his wife Georgia who would lie about the house all day in a hefty mess when she wasn't with Fannie Mae. She would tell him to kiss her behind whenever he'd want dinner or his clothes laundered. Sometimes she would return home after a three-day spree and Nosetrouble would get ill and threaten to hang himself. I dozed off while he recited his grand strategy, and when I awoke he too had fallen asleep, curled up in one of the basket chairs and coddling a Leadbelly album. Our slumber was disturbed by quick giggling coming from behind the door. I opened it and was greeted by Mrs. Nosetrouble and my wife. Their dresses were rumpled. Their breaths stank of strong drink.

"Where's the fuken grocery money, bitch?" I asked Fannie Mae. "You were supposed to buy: two pounds of neck bones, marked-down day-old bread, a can of beans, four cartons of beer, a bottle of milk, a bunch of greens, a can of Spam, a pound of rice, coffee, a pound of hog maws—with what I gave you."

Georgia walked past me and into the living room where her husband sat fuming.

"Where did you get the money to go drinking with Fannie Mae?" he asked her.

"I pawned that tiny black case you're always playin' wif."

He caught her with an uppercut which sent her flying against the bookcase, spilling pamphlets and documents to the floor. She bellowed like an animal whose paw has just been crushed by a fire truck. Nosetrouble stood triumphantly over his wife.

"If you have spent that grocery money, I will kick the livin' shit out of you!" I continued to Fannie Mae.

Fannie Mae stepped back from me a few paces. "You lay a hand on me, I'll see to it that your behind is shoved under the mothafukin' jail."

Nosetrouble dropped to his knees and embraced Georgia. He told her how much he loved her and said that he had lost his temper and that I had prompted him to take drastic action which was totally out of keeping with his character.

I started to maul the kat but my hands were full. Fannie Mae bolted for the elevator door, slamming the door of the Nosetroubles' apartment in my face.

In the hall I waited for the elevator to rise again. From the apartment I could hear effusive squeaks and groans. Finally I reached the bottom floor and ran across the projects grounds, my arms swinging from side to side in front of me.

I emerged from the building just as Fannie Mae shut the door to our apartment. With strength that surprised me, I tore the door from its hinges and slammed it to the floor of the hall.

"What's come over you, man! You lost yo mind or something?"

I walked toward Fannie Mae, forcing her against the wall, and tried to sink my claws into her throat.

"This will be the last time you spend my hard-earned money on *Screen Gems* magazines and liquor," I growled.

She pried herself loose from my grasp and ran into the hall.

"HELP/ LAWDY/ JESUS/ MOSES/ ELIJAH/ DANIEL/ MERCY/ MAMMA/ DADDY/ HELP ME! DA MAN DONE GONE APESHIT!"

M/ and F/Neighbor's eyes appeared through the peephole of their apartment. Once outside, she yelled up to me at the window.

"I'm goin' over to my father's house. You as looney as dey come. Don't try to follow me neither."

"Here's a gift for your grandmother," I snarled, throwing a broom out of the window which landed at her feet.

That night a phone call from the Grand Exalted Ruler of the Elks Ret. Himself.

"Uh, O. You done gone and did it now, Doopeyduk. You 'sturbed my daughter so with yo conniptions dat she got upset and nearly slipped into the oven. She is suffering from burns and shock and had to be took to the Harry Sam Hospital. If you ever upset my daughter again, I'm gone send my clean-jawed and bald assassins after you. Dey don't eat pork as you know and dey make their wives wear dresses whose hems reach their ankles. So dey is in good condition." (Click!)

I walked to the window of my apartment. The full moon. I marveled.

I wore my cap over my eyes and gloves to conceal my claws. I reached the hospital where my mother and father were sitting in the lobby. My mother had enough chinchillas on her to weigh down a whole garment pusher's detail. My father wore a Petrocelli suit and toyed with his hat.

"We tried to raise you right, Bukka. But you never know how dey's going to turn out, as Mrs. Nosetrouble just said up in Fannie Mae's room."

I was reticent. "Could you tell me where the room is?"

"It's over there, but Bukka, we just gone have to pray for you. By the way," she continued, "Fannie Mae told me a while back you got a raise of five dollars at the hospital. Least you could do is turn me and your daddy on to a few dollars a week to help us add that garage to the new house we just bought to rent out."

"I was demoted, so I can't help you out."

"I knew he'd never amount to anything," she said to my father as I walked toward the entrance of the ward where the indigent patients were placed. Nurses' aides were putting bundles of soiled sheets into dumbwaiters. Some women in flimsy robes held together by safety pins were walking slowly down the aisle holding their groins. Nurses were carrying cups with pills to beds which were emitting rough guttural sounds.

Fannie Mae lay in the middle of the room with dark circles under her eyes. Tubes protruded from her body as if she had taken root. A bottle hung next to her bed where she fed intravenously. Her face was sallow and cheeks sunken.

The nurse said, "Don't stay too long. She has been delirious and is under heavy sedation but I think she will recognize you."

Fannie Mae batted her eyes then looked up at me. "HELP! HELP! HE GONE VISCERATE ME. HE—"

"Calm down," I said. "I just wanted to apologize for disturbing you so."

"Well, Grandmama said dat da hoodoo had been put on you 'cause you were a loser and a creep and nothing would ever come of you. She told me I should leave you."

My mouth quivered as I started to speak. The orderlies and nurses' aides stopped and moved in closer to the bed. Their arms folded, their ears cupped. The lab people dumped ol people off carts and left women's breasts hanging before the X-ray machines. Patients were left with scissors in their wounds as surgeons moved into the room and closed in about the bed. One man who was about to be declared dead got up and came into the room arm in arm with his priest. Crowds of people were perched atop carts, sitting in window sills, jostling and maneuvering for a better view. There was silence when I spoke.

"I apologize for frightening you. I lost my head. I have not been keeping abreast of my Nazarene studies." I stopped and put a paw in my mouth. My voice was sounding like the growling of an animal.

She lifted her head and said, "Did you bring cigarettes, chump? After all, we lay in dese beds in our own mess, rats leap into da nightstands, and down below some of da po' patients are moved into some room and come back wif dey legs all cut off, even though they was only in here for da whoopin' cough. You have to ring da bell for hours jess to get a drink of water. We need a smoke or we will go crazy."

"Filter tip or plain?" I asked in a deep croaking voice.

The crowds of people fell from their positions in laughter. Men doubled up on the floor and howled. I charged through the crowd and my cap fell off. Women in the halls screamed, as I swung over the staircase and into the street. There were air-drill alerts, people running. A sound truck announced: A NATIONAL EMERGENCY OF HIGHEST IMPORTANCE/ THE HARRY SAM JOHN IS STOPPED UP/ EVERYONE GO INSIDE OFF THE STREETS/ WE REPEAT . . .

I ran. Convoys of plumbers were moving across the bay in battleships with rags sticking from their back pockets. They were armed with monkey wrenches and pliers and hammers. I continued to run. A truck pulled up to the park and cans of dead newsreels were dumped. I ran. The old men dropped to their knees, crossed themselves and cheered for the holiday. They swung their pails and walked somberly from the park.

Through the field glasses one could see the judges, generals and His Excellency Nancy Spellman tumbling down the slopes of the island toward their limousines while clammy fingers were adjusting their gas masks. I kept on running—galloping on my hooves like the wind.

PART II

An Old Woman Kidnaps Checkers

And I ran until I stumbled over a man who was lying face down in the street. My heels spun as I flew into a row of garbage cans causing the lids to tumble clanging into the gutter. In front of the spent form rested a giant ball of light manure. Thinking that the man might be ill, I went over to him and tugged at his armpits. Lying next to his body was a piece of luggage upon which were pasted stickers with the names of several Western capitals. Aroused, he slowly turned over and rubbed his eyes. I recognized him at once! It was my old professor from the Harry Sam College, U2 Polyglot, working out some empirical problems of his paper, "The Egyptian Dung Beetle in Kafka's 'Metamorphosis.'"

"Bukka, my boy," he said as he sat upright in the street. "What are you doing outdoors during this grave crisis? All citizens have been advised to remain inside with their shades drawn and their fingers crossed."

"I was on my way home before I fell into you, professor," I answered.

He lit a pipe which he removed from the luggage at his side and continued to examine me. "My boy," he finally said, "you look a little weak. I mean, those pointed ears and hooves. What are you trying to do, get on a quiz show or something?"

I told him of the setbacks I had received since leaving the Harry Sam College: the fights with Fannie Mae; my physical and spiritual deterioration; my increasing doubts as to the validity of the Nazarene discipline.

When he heard the last of these downcomings, the pipe nearly fell from his lips. "You've not kept up with the faith! That indeed is serious. You must get right down on your knees and repeat after me."

The thinned tweed of U2 Polyglot's knees met the street and I knelt next to him as he chanted: "HARRY SAM does not love us. If he did, he would come out of the John and hold us in his lap. We must walk down the street with dem signs in our hands. We must throw back our heads and loosen our collars. We must bawl until he comes out of dere and holds us like it was before the boogeyman come on the scene and everybody went to church and we gave each other pickle jars each day and nobody had acne or bad breath and cancer was just the name of a sign."

The professor—after the manner of the Nazarene Bishops—lifted his nose from the street with great dignity. He then looked both ways and whispered into my ear: "Look, Bukka. I know that you've been afflicted with the hoodoo. That's no disgrace; why in the 'bad ol

days' they took the hoodooed, bound their paws, gagged
them and made them lie on straw mats. But in this
enlightened period, we take a more *scientific* view of
this disease and that my boy is precisely what it is—a
disease and not a curse."

He shook his head sadly, then said, "The life of a
scholar has its ups and downs, Bukka. We try to lift
the spiritual sights of mankind and what do we get?
These piddling allowances from the state for projects in
the humanities, such as the one in which I'm now engaged. The grant I received for pushing this goddamn
ball all over Europe is not enough to keep me in good
pipe tobacco—so I've taken to a little hustlin'* on the
side. You see, there's this ol woman with two bricks
for breasts who was taking conjure lessons through the
mail under the Mojo Power Retraining Act. The other
day while experimenting she came upon a recipe for
allaying the symptoms and even curing advanced stages
of hoodoo fever. I've been selling the stuff like hotcakes
in Europe, scene of mysterious hoodoo epidemics, and I
get five per cent on each bottle sold."

He removed a bottle from the luggage which I tried
to wrest from his hand, so eager was I to return to my
normal self.

"Not so fast," he said, gripping the bottle. "That'll be
five mazumas."

I shoved the bills into his hand which he totaled—
licking his thumb after each count. I unscrewed the bottle's cap and poured the solution down my throat. I became itchy and nauseous. Convulsing and retching, I

* Readers will note that U2 Polyglot is quite adept at the use of
slang. This is because his position at the Harry Sam College was
that of Chairman of the Department of American Studies.

held my hips with crossed arms. My nostrils bristled
from the sharp odor of the fluid and hair began to fall
away from my body. Fangs dropped from my mouth,
and falling into the street, broke into fine crystals. My
feet began to shake involuntarily as if stricken.

"Thank you, professor," I said to U2 Polyglot, as I
began to feel a new lease on life.

"That's all right," he said, lighting up his benevolent
eyes, those soft eyes which looked like chick-peas. "I
still have faith that you will become a fine Nazarene
Bishop, one of these days; I only hope that I will be
able to follow your career."

I was about to bid him farewell when suddenly a
jeep full of Screws pulled up next to the ball whose
greenish-brown flakes shone in the moonlight. One Screw
stood up in the vehicle as soon as it screeched to a halt
and aimed a turkey musket at our heads.

"What is this crap?" he shouted. "Why aren't you
citizens indoors like everybody else? Haven't you been
informed of the curfew?"

I was scared to death, but the professor seemed un-
perturbed as the Screw's fingers fidgeted with the trigger
of the turkey musket. U2 Polyglot removed some officious-
looking papers bearing the greenish-brown seal of HARRY
SAM from his vest pocket. The Screw's eyes popped
after he inspected them. He grinned meekly, then snapped
to a stiff salute and clicked his heels. "Forgive me, Your
Excellency, for interfering with a top-secret project."

"That's all right," U2 Polyglot replied. "We must all
be on guard against enemies of HARRY SAM."

The Screw saluted, then shouted something to the other
four who were huddled together in the back seat of

the jeep. The vehicle jerked forward then backward and skidded around the corner on two wheels.

"Well, Bukka," the professor said. "I have to get back to work. Take it easy, kid." With this said, he lodged his nose in the ball of manure and with aplomb and correctness began pushing it down the street. I waved, until U2 Polyglot became a dark speck on the horizon.

The projects were settled in heavy gloom. Hundreds of candles flickered behind the yellow curtains of the narrow cubicles. The sirens wailed throughout the area and men holding flashlights trotted through the streets. The Nazarene apprentices from the universities—looking like sick dust mops—were dispensing coffee and doughnuts to the volunteers. I went into my apartment and turned on radio station UH-O. Reports of the crisis in the Harry Sam John were coming in from all over the world:

> Because of the grave crisis in the Harry Sam John the Pope has called in all Bingo cards. Appearing on the balcony of his Vatican apartment and waving his crooked finger over a restless throng, the Pontiff said that "under no circumstances would last week's Bingo results be revealed."
>
> A milling crowd booed as the Swiss guards rolled wheelbarrows up to the Sistine Chapel and dumped tons of Bingo cards. Early-morning raids were staged in key Latin American cities as bootleg Bingo games were broken up. On Mulberry Street in Lower Manhattan, mobs pelleted police, hooted and cursed as they yelled: "Give us Bingo or shoot us." Although a spokesman has said that last week's Bingo results are walled up in a secret room in the Vatican protected by three Spanish cardinals, informed sources here say they've

been passed on to the American ambassador. They are: B6, I16, N26, FREE, G33, O43. The State Department has issued a flat denial.

I shut off the radio and began to repair the house which was still in shambles from my strife with Fannie Mae. The lamps were overturned. Ashtrays lay scattered on the rug and chairs were broken into splinters. Dead plants lay in soiled spots near broken vases. I stretched my arms, yawned, then went into the kitchen and downed a bottle of beer. I then went into the bedroom, removed my clothes, curled up into a ball, threw the covers over my head and went to sleep.

At about twelve o'clock loud reports of gunfire came from the island. I ran to the window and raised the shades. Shadows moved behind the curtains of the other apartments. Frightened tenants looked out of their windows and across the bay to the Harry Sam Motel which stood at the summit of his mountain. The sky above the motel blazed a bright red, lighting up the night as if it were day. The sign on the roof of the motel blinked on and off rapidly: EATS EATS EATS EATS EATS EATS EATS EATS EATS EATS. I hurried back to bed with both arms outstretched and hit the sheets with such a thud the planks nearly collapsed.

People are walking on the deck of a ship. Seated in two chairs are Dick and Pat Nixon and their dog, Checkers. Dick is signing autographs for a group of maimed war veterans who stand before the family, some on stumps and some on crutches and walking canes. One mutilated G.I. is blind and he bumps into the deck chair jarring Pat Nixon who smiles and returns to her knitting. Two other men appear. They are dressed fancier than the others. One says, "It was much better in Egypt at the time of the two cities, Matthew. The artists and dreamers lived in one and the slaves lived in the other." They walk to the rail and lean over looking below at the hundreds of hands holding paddles which stick from the portholes. One man removes a small bottle of acid from his pocket, unscrews the top and pours it on one of the hands. The flesh of the hand falls away and drops into the water. A piercing scream is heard below. The man's companion falls to the deck and banging his fists on the boards, dies laughing. Pat Nixon is not amused; she walks over to the rail and jots down their names. She then returns to her chair and sits down in a huff. An ol woman appears. Under her armpit she carries the Christmas issue of the Reader's Digest (stars, snow and reindeer on a blue cover). The lead article is "Should Dolphins Go Steady—33 Parents Reply." She stoops over and pretends to pat Checkers. The Nixons and the war veterans are charmed by the sweet ol soul. Suddenly the ol woman swoops Checkers into her arms and splits. The Nixons and the soldiers hobbling on their crutches and artificial limbs give chase shaking their fists and shouting.

In the stateroom there is an orchestra of men in white dinner jackets entertaining ol generals with songs from the "bad ol days." Songs such as "Faraway Places with Strange-Sounding Names" and strains of "Don't Fence Me In" are heard. Betty Grable appears through the curtains to thunderous applause. She bends a knee and holds her left hip with her left hand and with the other hand touches the back of her hair—which is arranged in an upsweep; the ol men put their fingers between their teeth and whistle. Others stamp their feet and say, "Hip, hip, hooray."

A crash is heard outside the stateroom as a deck chair overturns. The ol woman appears at the entrance holding a yipping dog. She speeds across the room in her black sneakers knocking the ol generals from their tables. The stateroom empties as the ol men chase the widow executioner holding the cocker spaniel being chased by the Nixons followed by . . . or is it the war veterans chasing the generals who are chasing the Nixons? Anyway, the Nixons and the soldiers enter the stateroom. Betty Grable says, "They went thataway." The entire string section rises with their violin bows pointed to the direction of the other exit. The ol woman jumps to the top of the rail and holding her nose and the dog under her armpit dives into the drink and starts making it out to sea plowing the water with lusty breast strokes. Tricky Dick and the Mrs. followed by the soldiers are not far behind.

Betty Grable's chance for a comeback has been spoiled. She sits on the stage brooding, eating a Hershey bar and holding her jaw in her hand. Not to be outdone she gets up and says to the orchestra, "Come on, boys." The ol woman followed by the four men followed by the generals followed by the Nixons followed by the war veterans followed by Betty Grable followed by the orchestra swim toward the skyline in single file.

Dawn. Only a few volleys of gunfire are heard. I went to the window and raised the shades. An object appears at the mouth of one of the statues of the nineteenth President of the United States resting upon the imposing slope of Sam's Island. It is a white coffin which plunks into the bay. Another coffin appears. Then 4–5–10–14. The dingy cloud above the motel lifts. The sun shows through. At eleven A.M. there is a bulletin.

LATEST ATTEMPT TO JAM UP THE WORKS FOILED. ECLAIR PORKCHOP A HERO AS HE ACTS AS A HUMAN PUMP DISLODGING THE BANTAM ROOSTER FEATHERS CONSPIRATORS USED TO PLUG THE PIPES.

Things were returning to normal in the big not-to-be-believed nowhere. Walking through the projects to work I saw women trudging to the laundromats with baskets of dirty clothes. The men were stepping onto the chartered buses that would take them to the Harry Sam Ear Muffle Factory. Carrying brown bags full of sandwiches, they walked resignedly with their heads bowed. The children were merrily playing on the amusement truck; romping over the stainless steel gnomes, giraffes and jackals and little trickster figures with long noses and stocking caps on their heads.

When I reached the hospital I unlocked the door with my passkey and went into the lounge of the psychiatric unit which was used by the orderlies to change their clothes and relax on their coffee breaks. Two orderlies were conversing while another stared at the center page of a popular men's magazine which displayed a cadaver that was studying esoteric pharmacology at the N/School of Social Research.

"Yeah, it gone be a good break for somebody. Say the man come in lass night jessa screamin' and hollin'. Nurse Rosemary D Camp promises that the orderly chosen to take care of him will get a five-dollar raise. Sho hopes it bees me."

"Me too," said the other orderly, turning to me as I buttoned my short-sleeved white shirt. "Doopeyduk, you heah 'bout the man come in the hospital last night jessa screamin' and hollin'?"

"No," I answered coldly, not wishing to encourage fraternizing with the other orderlies from Soulsville whom I considered lowly ruttish lumpen.

"Say he come in lass night talkin' all out hee head.

Nurse Rosemary D Camp say who evah takes care o him good gone get a five-dollar raise."

There was a rap at the door of the orderlies' lounge. The men hurriedly stamped out their cigarettes and pushed the fumes through the opened window. Nurse Rosemary D Camp peeked in and her singsong voice said, "Mr. Doopeyduk, will you please come into my office?"

"Yes, Mrs. Nurse Rosemary D Camp," I replied nervously. "I'll be down as fast as I can."

When I entered the room she invited me to sit in a chair next to her desk. She was a fat woman with a round doll-like face with rouged cheeks. Her arms were thick as hams and showed small dents here and there from the shoulders to her fingers resting on the desk. Hanging from beneath her cap were long twisted pigtails; pinned to the blouse of her uniform she wore a purple orchid upside down.

"Mr. Doopeyduk," she began, "mishaps are bound to happen in an operation such as the one in which we are engaged on Unit Five. So I think that we might have been a little harsh with you after your accident with the patient who was here a few weeks ago." She smiled at me while I squirmed in the chair. "Otherwise we've found that you've been conscientious in many other matters arising in the course of your duties. So we've decided, Mr. Doopeyduk, to give you a special assignment for this evening. Your performance on this assignment will indicate to us whether you're ready for larger responsibilities."

"Mrs. Nurse Rosemary D Camp," I said, "I will certainly do my best to warrant your confidence."

"Good, then," she replied. "This is your assignment. There was an old man admitted to the floor last night. I'm afraid he's delirious and raving. We want you to get samples so that we can analyze them. He has meningitis and typhoid complicated by double pneumonia. You will be given a surgeon's mask and we want you to give him lots of fluids and rub his back with powder. Then at the conclusion to your shift we want you to make out a report on him."

I jumped to my feet and started for the door.

"One minute, Mr. Doopeyduk, we have a little surprise for you." She opened the drawer and pulled out A GOLDEN BEDPAN WITH MY INITIALS ENGRAVED ON THE BOTTOM.

I was all choked up. "I don't know what to say, Mrs. Nurse Rosemary D Camp."

"That's all right, Mr. Doopeyduk," the nurse said. "We're sure that you will prove yourself worthy."

I opened the door, knocking over the three orderlies who had their ears fastened to the keyhole. Ignoring them I walked to the old man's room with my nose upturned and holding the bedpan engraved with my initials.

The old man had been placed in a secluded ward. He lay under an oxygen tent in the bed, next to which was a floor lamp exuding a soft violet glow. He wore a damp waist-length nightgown and his bony knees were propped up under his hamstrings by pillows. His wrists were bound to the side rail and his eyes were two black dots. A thin layer of skin stretched around the small skeletal outlines of his face. I read the chart which hung at the foot of his bed.

Man: White male gave his name as Roger Young Ist.
About 89 years old. Admitted to the floor at
2:00 A.M. Only possession—a musty can of newsreel entitled *Versailles 1919.* He fought five orderlies for the can yelling, "Gimmie back my
newsreel, I want my newsreel." Scratched and
bit and spat on them until he was subdued with
vesperin. Went to sleep about 5 A.M.
Diagnosis: Schizoid with paranoid tendencies. Keeps
muttering, "The Huns raping the nuns."

I changed the man every five minutes until the corner
of the room was filled with sticky wet sheets. I applied
the powder and gave him a rubdown.

He finally went off to sleep. The room was quiet. I
sat in a chair next to his bed leafing through a magazine.
At about 6:30 P.M. he suddenly rose, lurched forward
and pointed a long bent finger toward the open door of
the room.

"Save me! They're in the door! The Free-Lance Pallbearers are in the door! Look, look! The long frock coats
and shiny black boots, the black box! It's them! They're
going to try to take ol Roger Ist away from here! Please
save me, ooooo, save me, no! Get back! Get back! Arra!
Ggggg! Grggrrrrgrrg! Rrgrgrgrrrrrrrrrgrgrrrgrrrrrrr g . . .
. . . . r . . . . !"

I ran through the door of the room and into the
nurses' quarters. "Mrs. Nurse Rosemary D Camp! Please
hurry—the old man is hallucinating; he seems to be having an attack of some sort."

All the orderlies and doctors ran clomping down the
hall toward the room. But it was too late. The old man
had given up the ghost.

We washed him, wrapped him in a shroud and placed

him in a basket. He was then rolled into the morgue and placed in an ice-cold tray. (One of the morgue attendants was to say later that upon making a routine inspection he found the corpse holding the can of newsreel in a death clutch.)

It was the end of my shift. I filled out the report on the deceased and gave it to the nurse. "Thank you, Mr. Doopeyduk," she said. "You made the poor ol man's last hours as comfortable as possible. We'll be calling on you in the future for more tasks like these."

One of the orderlies helped me with my coat. "I will do my best to justify your faith in me," I told the nurse. (I detected a snicker from the orderly who was helping me with the garment, but I ignored him, attributing it to jealousy on his part.) I walked out into the streets of Soulsville toward home. The crisis over, the convoys of plumbers in battleships headed from Harry Sam Island toward the pier. They leaned over the rails of the ships guffing down the hot dogs and beer.

In Soulsville banners hung over the street. WELCOME SOULSVILLE'S OWN ECLAIR PORKCHOP. Barricades had been set up and Screws linked hands holding back the crowd which had come out to greet the newly appointed bishop. They were not to be disappointed because the parade turned out to be quite a spectacle. I lined up with the crowd to get a better view of the goings-on.

The first car in the procession was a big sleek Rolls-Royce. The body of the car was painted lavender and the hood was a frieze depicting the Nazarene apocalypse. It was painted in wild wiggy colors.

It showed HARRY SAM the dictator and former Polish used-car salesman sitting on the great commode. In

his lap sat a businessman, a Nazarene apprentice and
a black slum child. These figures represented the Just.
Standing on each side of the dictator were four washroom attendants. In their hands they had seven brushes,
seven combs, seven towels, and seven bars of soap, a
lock of Roy Rogers' hair and a Hershey bar. Above the
figures float Lawrence Welk champagne bubbles. Below
this scene tombstones have been rolled aside and the
Nazarene faithful are seen rising in a mist with their
hands reaching out to the figure sitting on the commode.

There were purple velvet curtains on the windows of
the car. Through the drapes of the back window was
a wrinkled yellow hand. On one of the fingers was a
large sardonyx ring.

It was Nancy Spellman, Chief Nazarene Bishop. It
was a crime punishable by death to look at him directly
so the people bowed their heads and closed their eyes.
Following the automobile on foot were the Nazarene
Bishops. They wore Dobbs hats and double-breasted suits
with ball-point pens sticking from their pockets. Carna-
tions were pinned to their lapels.

Next came a black Pierce-Arrow. A chauffeur's velvet
glove gripped the car wheel. He sat next to a bottle of
Fleischmann's which was as large as his body from the
waist up. A spindly old woman sat next to him waving
a long cigarette holder and dangling her leg over the
car door.

She was holding her hands together responding to
the cheers of the crowd. In the rear half of the car,
through the roof, some plastic antlers appeared. The
woman wore a green satin dress under a black bolero
jacket. She wore a diamond ring on every other finger
of her hands. Sparkling green mascara was smeared to

the edge of her plucked-out eyebrows. Her hair was
tinted blue-silver and frizzed in a permanent wave. A
white ermine stole with black tails was thrown across
her neck and dripped down her back. A heavy beaded
necklace hung to her stomach. It was my father-in-law's
mother and the bitch was dressed to kill. The automobile
pulled to a halt. The chauffeur climbed out and went to
the rear of the car and opened the trunk. Children who
were poking their noses through the spokes of the tires
were shooed away.

He brought a case to the side of the car and gave
her a bottle. She held up a bottle of the anti-hoodoo
lotion. Suddenly da hoodooed leaped from alleys and
jumped from the windows of fleabag hotels, and dropped
their forks and Chicago caps (which had been pulled
down over their eyes) into their bean soups in restaurants
as they left trails of screaming waitresses who tossed
check pads into the air and jumped on tables, and the
beasts bent bars of jails and hurdled the lamps of police
stations, and nurses shrieked disbelief as da hoodooed
knocked over trays in hospitals where they were under-
going the hoodoo kick, and they loped from the beds
and toppled confessional booths in churches where they
were being expunged of the fever—causing the priests
to fling themselves upon the coins which had spilled from
falling collection baskets, and da hoodooed bolted
through the doors of churches, hospitals, jails, cellar
apartments, jumped from rooftops, leaped out of alley-
ways, and jaunting to the forefront of the crowd snatched
bottles from her hand before she could deliver her pitch.
The chauffeur held fistfuls of dollar bills they slapped into
his hands as the old woman stood up in the seat of the

Pierce-Arrow, rolled up her sleeves and ran down her game.

"Come and get your anti-hoodoo lotion! Get rid of those ugly fangs, that tired hair. Be a delight to the womenfolk."

While she went into her thing I walked to the rear of the car to examine the plastic antlers of my father-in-law. I pressed my nose against the window and saw my father-in-law dressed in a tuxedo and resting his hand upon an ebony cane. He was swinging the antlers from side to side while talking to some ladies in cotton dresses who remembered him as the head of the colored Elks in 1928.

"How you, Miss Lucy?" he drawled, giving one woman a limp handshake and exposing his gold teeth. "How's the youngins? Hopes they's fine."

"Father-in-law, father-in-law," I shouted. He turned to the rear window and momentarily flashed anger; but remembering the women standing next to the car, he spoke for their edification.

"Well, my goodness, if it ain't my son-in-law. What you wont, dear son-in-law?" The women smiled at this exhibition of family affection. He rolled the car window down and beckoned me to come closer. "Look, my man," he said out of the hearing range of his admirers. "Make it. It'll mess up what you might call our 'image' if we are seen in the company of an orderly." I fell back to the curb and shoved my hands into my orderly's uniform which was still soiled from the old man's juices.

All the merchandise sold, the old woman had returned to her place next to the chauffeur. She clapped her hands and the car moved on. The car was followed by a battalion of old men wearing derbys and aprons with mystic

signs sewn on them. Others were wheeled along by
nurses who held up the old men's arms occasionally so
that they could respond to the good wishes of the festive
crowd. They were part of that celebrated contingent who
in glittering ceremony underneath the watchful eyes of
the founders of the nation—who wore frills on their
wrists and fake moles on their cheeks—stood in solemn
silence as their leader, my father-in-law, knelt, un-
sheathed his sword and kissed Calvin Coolidge's ass. At
that time a minor stir was created when a protocol officer
ran up and pulled my father-in-law from the President.
He said that the proper procedure was to pull aside one
flap and kiss the President between the cheeks instead
of smacking the Chief of State all over his bottom like
some kind of madman. My father-in-law nearly went to
blows with the protocol officer for embarrassing him before his following and all those "fine white peoples." But
the President saved the day, pulling up his trousers
and saying, "We Americans are known for our informal-
ity."

For saving my father-in-law from a humiliation that
could have set back "the struggle" fifty years, *Ebony*
magazine hailed Calvin Coolidge as the second eman-
cipator.

The old men were roundly applauded by the onlookers.
Suddenly a woman fell into the arms of a man standing
behind her. Another woman swooned. People began dropping like flies. A rank stench filled the air and the spectators held handkerchiefs to their noses and puked on each
other. Up ahead was a 1938 Oldsmobile flanked by a
V-shaped entourage of Screws on motorcycles. The Screws
wore gas masks. Standing in the back seat of the car
and wearing damp peppermint-striped pajamas and a

cone-shaped hat was none other than Eclair Porkchop, newly crowned Bishop of Soulsville, direct from his negotiations with Dictator HARRY SAM, former Polish used-car salesman. Those who could withstand the odor which filled the street like quicksand fumes bowed their heads or held up their babies to receive Eclair Porkchop's blessing. The Bishop lighted from the automobile and walked on a red carpet toward the door of the Church of the Holy Mouth. Some young men on the sidelines teased the Bishop by playfully pinching his buttocks. He spun away, sticking out his hand like a quarterback dodging tackles. He executed pirouettes, arabesques, grands jetés saying, "Stop, hee, hee, that tickles. Now stop, now, hee, hee."

Those who could take the stench followed him until he was swallowed by the door of the church. He was shadowed by those men HARRY SAM assigned to protect his bishopric. They wore pantaloons and brogans. They were stripped to the waist and peering through the terrifying eyeholes of their masks they beat back the crowd with their whips.

All at once a man elbowed his way through the crowd. The hem of a long vicuña coat reached his ankles. He paced up and down in front of the crowd with his hands behind his back. Once in a while he glanced at his watch. He had a heavy mustache and a cigar jutted aggressively from between his teeth. A dwarf hunch-backed Negro ran through the crowd and joined the man. The Negro wore a raccoon coat and a straw hat. He waved a pennant which read "Fisk 1950." Underneath his arm he carried a small black case. "Hurry up, hurry up," the first man said to the dwarf as the little fellow opened the case, pulled out a mouth organ and began to play the Protestant hymn "The Old Rugged Cross." It was the mad slum lord Irving Gooseman and his Negro dwarf assistant Slickhead Fopnick. Irving cupped his thick red trap and addressed the crowd.

"All you little pretties and swingers of Soulsville, this is your main man Irving Gooseman and Slickhead Fopnick telling you all the bargains at the USURA pawnshop. No cash down—all you have to have is a gig. Take as long as you wont, all you souls, little pretties and swingers, boppers and groovers. Come on over to the store and look at some fine jools, dig some blond coffee tables and some zebra-skin couches. Now as an introduction to USURA pawnbrokers, we offer you a record that no home should be without. It's historical. It's edjoocational. It's a credit to you people. A forty-five disc of the historic meeting between HARRY SAM and Soulsville's own Eclair Porkchop: 'A Meeting of Titans.' Just so that you can get a sample of this dignified recording, we're going to play a little bit of it." With this he pulled a folding stand from beneath his overcoat, set it up and mounted a small victrola on the top. He put the needle on the record and soon the voices of the two leaders could be heard.

AWWWWW, DO IT TO ME. AWWWWWW BABY. DO IT TO ME. WHERE DID YOU GET THAT LONG THING? MY MY O LORD, DON'T STOP, DON'T STOP. HELPLEASE DON'T STOP. DO IT THIS WAY. DO IT THAT WAY. OOOOOO MY MY MY YUM YUMMY OOOO . . .

The sleep-in maids, porters and redcaps, hustlers, junkies, and Nazarene apprentices threw nickels, dimes, and quarters into the basket. All at once two Screws appeared around the corner and spotting the mad slum lord and Slickhead gave chase. Irving and Fopnick got their gear together and jumped into a T-Model Ford which was parked behind the crowd. The car rattled and bustled so, a door fell from its hinges and into the street. Smoke and oil spouted furiously from its radiator cap.

The Ford sped toward the railroad tracks where the eight-thirty express of the B.&O. Railroad was bearing down on the crossroads like gangbusters. The Screws were hot on the pair's trail, speeding in a jeep. Some of them were standing on the runners firing BB pellets at the car wheels. The crowd watched as the train came nearer and nearer and nearer and nearer (drum rolls) until the old T-Model just slipped across the tracks almost running down an old woman in white who was dripping wet and holding a yelping mutt by the scruff of the neck as she dashed across the road on the other side of the tracks. The Screws were left jumping up and down in the jeep, throwing their helmets into the road shoulders, tearing out their hair and slapping their fists against their foreheads in frustration as a lot of dumb numbers on boxcars whizzed by at one hundred miles an hour.

PART III

Rutherford Birchard Hayes Is Thrown from a Horse

Fannie Mae did not return from the hospital. Instead I received a summons in the mail, directing me to appear before Judge Whimplewopper on such and such a date in this incredible nightmare of a NOWHERE. Fannie Mae was demanding a separation on grounds of mental cruelty. Georgia Nosetrouble's name was scrawled above the line designated "witness." The receipt of this intelligence sunk me into deepest pall. I had failed my first test as a Nazarene apprentice on a quest in the grimy grim world of HARRY SAM, not-to-be-believed, out-of-sight, run from the low-down nasty room.

Now there would be hard decisions to make. First, I would have to yield my apartment because of a rule which forbade single people from dwelling in them. I decided to put my mind at ease by going to the newsreel theater in Soulsville. This proved to be my undoing.

En route to the movies I passed the amusement truck which was parked outside the projects during the day. Most of the children were merrily riding the swans, ponies and other animals. In between these figures stood dwarfs, gnomes and witches. A lone child had his arm around one of the dwarfs. He seemed to be weeping and moving his lips as if speaking to the mute figure.

"What's wrong, little tot?" I offered.

"He won't take me across the Black Bay like he said he was going to."

"Who won't?" I said, looking around me.

"He won't," the little boy continued, pointing to the long-nosed dwarf who had the jokers' smile painted on his face.

These kids today have the darndest imagination, I thought.

"He doesn't play fair. He took the rest of those kids over there and they play in gardens and fly like birds."

I sought to appease the tiny chap. "If ol meany won't play with you, here's a nickel. Play on one of the rides."

But instead of doing cartwheels over my gift, the little kid became indignant. "Why don't you leave us alone, you grown-up boozehound? Why don't ya go play pinochle or start a war or something? Who asked your opinion anyway?" he said, hugging the dwarf.

"Now see here, you little brat, apparently your father has never read the passage in the manual about how little Nazarenes are supposed to behave toward grownups. You should never deride the utterances of grownups. What you need is an ol-fashioned spanking." I yanked him from the dwarf, spun him around and brought my hand swiftly against his backside. The little kid howled as I walked away from the truck wringing my hands.

A distance from the truck I looked around. The kids were still playing on the rides and the little fellow had his arms around the dwarf's shoulders. He was rapidly moving his lips.

Long lines of customers wound around the block leading to the theater. They held packages of Camembert, Gouda, provolone, port salut, Liederkranz, Brie, Edam, bleu and cheddar cheese. You see, there were these furry creatures inside who over the years had developed a pretty sophisticated palate. So as not to be maimed, it was advisable for patrons to bring something along with which to entertain the critters. I dropped my block of Swiss at the box office and paid my fare.

The newsreel was an account of the previous week's events: the choking of SAM's valves by bantam roosters' feathers, the dislodging of these feathers by Rev. Eclair Porkchop and his subsequent coronation as Bishop of Soulsville. Finally SAM surrounded by his attendants, little men wearing white smocks and bow ties replete with the familiar butterfly pattern, appeared on the screen. Our leader's stomach swelled over the rim of his shorts like a drooping balloon. I applauded wildly but mine was the only applause. In fact I detected some snickers among members of the audience. The black rowdies in the front row began to heckle and catcall. A few even made wolf whistles. I rose from my seat and rushed down the aisle until I stood before the area where they were seated. With one hand resting on a hip and wagging my finger I gave them a "brutally frank" lecture, as the typists at several Civil Service offices are fond of saying.

"How dare you insult our sacred institutions, our cherished heritage, you roughnecks—you low-life rakes."

"Aw man, set yo behind down," came someone's gruff reply.

"Indeed, 'seat myself,' you reprobates," I continued, to the taunts of several ruffians seated in the front row. "When one hears subversive remarks, it is one's duty to report them! Why it says right here on page seventy-seven of the manual . . ." I demonstrated, removing the torn book of creeds from my tweed pocket.

"Are we going to listen to you, schmuck, or listen to the newsreels?" the owner yelled between the chawed black cigar which leaned from his fat lips. "Whaddaya tink runs this dump? Cheese? Now sit down or I'll have one of my bruisers kick you out!"

I ignored the owner who stood to the rear of the theater next to a short man who was waving a college pennant. Casting a shadow upon the movie screen with my person I unflinchingly stood my ground, taking on all comers. The theater seemed to heave and rock from the commotion caused by the indignant customers, as I defended our big klang-a-lang-a-ding-dong and antiseptic boplicity. Paper cups, yellow greasy popcorn, and candy wrappers rained upon my head. With the strong burning lungs of martyrdom I repeated my oath. "HARRY SAM does not love us—"

But before I could continue a rough hand gripped me by the shoulder and lifted me until I was kicking thin air. "I'll make a citizen's arrest upon the entire theater!" I shouted but was drowned out by the cheers of the audience who seemed delighted by my unceremonious exit. With guffaws and belly laughs coming from his garlic-smelling mouth, the usher threw me to the pavement outside the theater where I landed flat on my back-side. As I was being ejected, tussling up the aisle with the usher, I was to hear the owner comment to his assist-ant, "Got to hand it to him, Slickhead. He may be a crackpot but he's got a lot of chutzpah."

I started to report the entire incident to the Screws but seeing as how I was shoulder high in difficulties—what's the use, I thought, heading back to the Harry Sam Projects.

When I arrived at the bar outside the Harry Sam Projects, I was still smarting from the sound thrashing received at the usher's hands. The bar was a broken-down joint with a few scarred topped tables and an ol-fashioned stove with paws whose pipe disappeared into the roof.

Seated at the barstools were the workers from the Harry Sam Ear Muffle Factory. My M/Neighbor and Nosetrouble sat at a table in the back. Nosetrouble was talking in a spirited manner and M/Neighbor was nod-ding his head. This meant that they were discussing Nosetrouble's plot to get SAM. M/Neighbor had a pecul-iar-shaped head with a sharp curvature in the back of the skull which prompted many people to deride him with colorful names like "watermelon head" or "football head."

Nosetrouble's distinguishing features were a sharp jaw and receding hairline. He had the habit of narrowing his eyelids whenever he spoke of his plot to get SAM. He was wearing open-toed sandals, a boat-neck sweater, and corduroy slacks. When I approached the table they greeted me vigorously, pumping my hand. Nosetrouble ordered me a beer.

"Haven't seen you in a long time, Bukka Doopeyduk. Where you been hiding?" Nosetrouble began.

"I've been getting special assignments at the hospital and in my spare time I go over rather obscure passages in the Nazarene manual and make red pencil marks in the margins of the pages. Sometimes I meditate over these issues on long walks."

"You're still in dat bag, huh Bukka? Don't you know dat HARRY SAM is full of shit?" asked M/Neighbor.

I was shocked by M/Neighbor's newly acquired political acumen. But maintaining my cool I parried his rib. "I didn't know that you dabbled in politics, M/Neighbor, and if I recall correctly, it was YOU who viewed with consternation the remarks your son made about our self-made Pole and dauntless Plymouth-pusher who 'nobody could undersell.'"

"You got it wrong. Me and my son don't see eye to eye on some issues. I even keeked him out da house 'cause I found some reefers in his room. And he kept on wearin' tablecloths and started talkin' funnier than dat little white boy Joel O. he was palling around wit. But he's right on one thing. Da man do smell no matter which way you look at it. And since I became a leader of my people, me and Nosetrouble gone have it out wit dis man."

"Indeed, M/Neighbor," interjected Nosetrouble. "We can have none of the bourgeois decadence that your son and his little teeny boppers were into. It was plain nihilism. They seemed to be having a lot of fun with savage boo-ga-loo dancing and love feasts. It was tactically correct of you to get rid of the boy, M/Neighbor, and further—"

"How is Georgia Nosetrouble?" I said, not wishing to hear Nosetrouble's recital of 'ol speeches made by the famous dead' for which these remarks were usually an introduction.

"She left me a week ago. Didn't you know? They're at your father-in-law's new town house that the munitions manufacturers and Texas oil money bought him. She's become Fannie Mae's companion. I read in the society page of the *Amsterdam News* that they were leaving for Europe next week. You see, SAM has appointed your father-in-law ambassador to Luxembourg."

"Ambassador to Luxembourg!" I gasped. (What operators that ol man and his mother were.) "I'm sorry about that, Nosetrouble," I said, offering my condolences.

"No need. At first I was upset but now I spend most of my time organizing so I don't have enough time for self-pity. You see, we've formed a committee to get at the root of these mysterious child disappearances. We want to prod the Screws into some kind of action. Why, haven't you been listening to the splendid speeches M/Neighbor has been making on the radio? Didn't you see his picture in the *Deformed Demokrat* last week?"

"That's right," M/Neighbor added. "*Life* be here tomorrow and *Esquire* comin' down next week."

"You know, Bukka," Nosetrouble continued after a pause, "I wouldn't be surprised if your man HARRY SAM didn't have a hand in these disappearances."

Now I could put up with some of these seditious remarks, but this was a bit much. Beside myself with rage I jumped to my feet and banged the table so hard that the beer suds spilled into the laps of both M/Neighbor and Nosetrouble. They abandoned their composure and held each other.

"I REFUSE TO SIT HERE AND LISTEN TO YOU DAMN OUR LEADER LIKE THAT!"

"Aw knock it off," M/Neighbor responded. "You sound like a tool and lackey of the capitalist class, cha-cha-cha." Nosetrouble nodded approvingly, winking at me.

I held the sides of my head. My temples were pounding like crazy. I got up and slowly staggered out of the bar. The people sat at the tables with their hands over their ears and eyes bulging like gargoyles. Subversion was rife. Plots, subterfuge were the order of the day. What was to become of our beloved out-of-sight, our razz-a-ma-tazz and o-bop-she-bang? I contemplated these questions, walking aimlessly through NOW-HERE with my eyes downcast. I kicked a tin can from time to time and occasionally sighted Screws lining up teeny boppers and frisking them. Leaves swirled about the streets, low-bent trees hooted with abandonment. Dogs howled and I ducked the too-close-for-comfort swoop of vampire bats.

I had reached the Emperor Franz Joseph Park. The ol men—having completed a day of kissing jive frames— were filing through an arch which stood at its entrance. The Four Horsemen of the Apocalypse rode on the top with fierce-looking eagles perched upon their shoulders. Under the steady bombardment of the elements over the years, some of the sculpture had broken away from its base. The ground surrounding the arch was littered with the heads of the famous dead. The ol men shambled into the tenements and ol brownstones of the street which adjoined this park of cannon balls stacked in triangular heaps. Through the windows of the fleabag hotels which stood in this strange community, some of the ol men could be seen lined up for showers. Others sat in the lobbies of hotel after dismal hotel playing chess or watching a television film of Neville Chamberlain's airport speech which followed his conference with the Dictator. Still others leaned against the walls of several missions with bowls of soup in their hands. They watched with hawk eyes their possessions: the cans of film, flags and ladders which rested on the ground beside them.

A procession moved toward me from the other end of the street. It was composed of some elderly gentlemen who pushed carts filled with artifacts and relics. The leader of this parade was a wizened-faced creature dressed in a ragged World War I uniform. His cart contained some parched manuscripts belonging to Wilfred Owen, stacks of broken violin scrolls, some twisted marble toilet bases and a big rock, the only remnant of Hadrian's wall. When his wheelbarrow came along the spot where I stood he suddenly dropped it and pointed to me. Then frantically signaling the other men, he approached me. Now I might be a Nazarene apprentice but enough is enough. I wasn't prepared to take a similar beating to the one dished out at the theater so I picked up a lead pipe which lay on the sidewalk.

"Wait a minute," the man pleaded. "We mean you no harm. I merely wanted to introduce you to some friends of mine. My name is Aboreal Hairyman. In my heyday I was an itinerant preacher but now SAM has taken me out of retirement—taken me out of the trees in a way—and he's made me chief investigator in the case of the slashed mini-skirts and hip boots."

The other men applauded one of their own who had made good.

"Now gentlemen," Aboreal said, "it's not for me to take the limelight but rather this young colored lad standing here deserves your deepest gratitude."

"Wha hoppened? Come on, boss. Tell us wha hoppened?" asked the toothless many. The ol men loved tall tales, having little else to do with their time save play brinkmanship, mope over the "decadence" of the youth and empty their colostomy bags.

"You see," Aboreal Hairyman explained, "I was in attendance at the public cinema viewing some film of the uprising from which our leader emerged victorious and this young man debated some rabble who were speaking ill of the faith. I've not seen such a display of valor in all my years."

I was taken aback by all this notoriety and before I knew it I was bobbing on two shoulders as two of the men began to carry me through the streets. One of them pulled out a rusty trumpet and began to play the Marseillaise. Two others ran to the head of the procession and unfurled a banner which read "Buy Victory Bonds. The Nuns are Raping the Huns," and each holding an end they began to goose-step through the streets.

"Why don't we take him over to the Seventeen Nation Disarmament Conference Bar and buy him a drink?" Aboreal suggested. With Aboreal in the lead strutting proudly with his chest thrown out and his chin high our outlandish troupe shuffled up to the door of the Seventeen Nation Disarmament Conference Bar. A man came flying out through the swinging doors and landed in front of Aboreal's feet. He got up, brushed off his clothes and shaking his fist at the door shouted, "You'll see, you'll see, just like Munich. You'll see."

Tears streamed down his face as he, disillusioned, re-

moved his Mickey Mouse button from his chest and
angrily flung it into the gutter. We laughed good-na-
turedly and went inside the bar and soon were standing
at the rail drinking giant steins and eating onions and
horseradish on cheese. At the tables other ol men were
ordering from menus. One sat nude except for a boiled
vest and tall hat whose top had been ripped off.

"I'd like some cucumber soup, some jellied deer tongue
and some Berchtesgaden 1936," he requested of the
husky walrus-mustached waiter who stood at his table.

When all the mugs at the bar were filled to the
brim Hairyman raised his stein and proposed a toast.
"At ease, gentlemen. I want to introduce all of you to
Bukka Doopeyduk, a brave young apprentice who single-
handedly bore the assault of some of our detractors in
the public cinema yesterday. Without assistance he took
on those monsters behind us, who breathe fire into the
neck of our tired generation. Long live Seato Nato Cento
and the granny executioners in black sneakers."

The ol men clinked their glasses, took some robust
swigs and then sang a rousing chorus of "I'm a Yankee-
Doodle Dandy." Suddenly the half-nude man rose from
his chair and genitals swinging moved toward us.

"Gentlemen," he said in the Boris Karloff voice. "A
toast to Lenore!"

There was sheer silence until Aboreal Hairyman spoke
up. "Alfred," Aboreal consoled, putting a sympathetic
hand on the man's shoulder, "please don't start that
again."

"A toast to Lenore, dammit," the man insisted, rudely
pushing Aboreal's hand aside. "How can we forget New-
port? The milling young women just home from Radcliffe
shading themselves near the picnic baskets? The sump-

78   *The Free-Lance Pallbearers*

tuous melons on the tables and the brilliant conversation?"

One ol man waving his hands wept uncontrollably, pleading with the speaker, "Don't talk about it, Alfred. Please don't talk about it, boo, hoo, boo, hoo."

"O the boat races," he said, ignoring some of the weaker of the ol men who had dropped their heads to their tables. Their violently trembling fingers clutched the handles of their steins as the man went on. "I would walk about in my duck pants and blazer and sometimes we'd go clam-digging. O, if only I could have continued paying for her harpsichord lessons, things would have turned out different."

"It wasn't your fault, Alfred," Aboreal Hairyman whispered.

"My boy," the grief-stricken gentleman said, turning to me, "it would have never happened if Matthew and Waldo had remained to guard the gate. The villagers wouldn't have been able to . . ." But he trailed off and broke down. After a pause he looked up, and reaching inside the top of his hat, brought out a gold watch. He put the gold watch in my hands. "My boy, I want to give you this as a token from Lenore and the army of unalterable bores."

"O, no I can't, sir," I protested.

"No, take it," he insisted, then wheeled about and slowly returned to his deer tongue, cucumber soup, his Berchtesgaden. Another man came, hesitated, gave me a carton of Picayune cigarettes. Still another, a shiny spittoon. I was babbling with joy.

"O, gentlemen. This is much more than I deserve. I can't take your pension checks, your boxes of gold dust twins and the elbow baking soda."

Aboreal Hairyman reassured me. "Now my boy, we fossils will be very much rebuffed if you won't take our gifts. You deserve each and every one of them," Aboreal said in State Department redundance.

"I must go home now and study my Nazarene manual but I'll never forget this night."

"Three cheers for Bukka Doopeyduk. Hip, hip. . . . Hip, hip. . . . Hip, hip. . . ." The ol men waved as I left the quaint Seventeen Nation Disarmament Conference Bar of flickering gas lamps and beaded curtains. Mist rose from the cobblestone streets. Horse-drawn carriages moved in and out of the shadows. From the 1870 dining palace the ol men could be heard singing the haunting strains of a World War I favorite:

Roger Young Roger Young was the glory and the story
of the everlasting tires of the infantry who died for
you and me young Roger of the story and the everlasting
wires of the infant free lies the story and the glory
of you and me Roger Young who died in his veins and
the . . .

I was as happy as a lark when I arrived home. I put down the gifts and turned on radio station UH-O.

TRAPPED IN HOWARD JOHNSON'S FOR THE THIRTY-FIFTH DAY BY ANGRY HOUSEWIVES IN MOTORIZED GOLF CARTS: CHINAMENS REFUSE TO YIELD. VATICAN SEALED OFF AS BINGO CRISIS ENTERS FIFTH WEEK. POPE ASKS COMPROMISE. CHINESE CHECKERS ANYONE?

On each side of the steps leading into the courtroom was a statue of a white seal balancing a bright ball by the tip of its nose. Inside in the ceiling of the main hall was a dome of murals depicting episodes from the life of Rutherford Birchard Hayes. RBH pulling the pig-

tails of the first Chinese officials to be received in the
White House; RBH commenting on the size of their
buck teeth to two of his cronies who hold the little dip-
lomat's jaws apart for a better look; Rutherford Birchard
Hayes making a mad dash to get rid of the poker cards
and the bottle of Old Hickory as the First Lady, af-
fectionately known as "Lemonade Lucy," pokes her coal-
scuttle hat of green silk into the Cabinet room to an-
nounce that lemonade and Kool-Aid are being served;
Rutherford Birchard Hayes kicked in the head by a horse
on October 21, 1864, but intrepidly opening the Wichita
pickle fair the next day; Rutherford Birchard Hayes
giving colorful and quaint measles blankets to some Indians who proudly pose with their headdresses thrown
back and their noses in the air like snooty camels while
the President winks at his poker partners who—in on
the prank—stand off to the side of the reception slapping
their thighs and covering their grinning mouths. In the
center of the dome was a giant mural of Rutherford
Birchard Hayes surrounded by his eight children: Birchard Austin Hayes, James Webb Cook Hayes, Rutherford Platt Hayes, Joseph Thompson Hayes, George Crook
Hayes, Fanny Hayes, Scott Russell Hayes and Manning
Force Hayes. They stand with their mouths open as
Daddy holds a big round and firm cucumber between
his raunchy lips at the Wichita pickle fair, October 22,
1864.

Inside the court, the clerk called for the case which
was to precede mine. The participants were roughly
shoved through the door. They were surrounded by an
unusually heavy detachment of Screws. Masks had been
drawn over their heads and their wrists were bound
with rope. The Screws positioned the pair before Judge

Whimplewopper. Whimplewopper stood on three telephone books behind the bench. He was a natural-born
midget afflicted with an unusually long nose. In fact the
nose was so long that it became the subject of a series
of features in the *National Inquirer.*

It was very difficult for Whimplewopper to conduct
a normal courtroom because many of the nose's fans
would line up in the corridors of the courtroom to take
pictures and ask its opinion on the length of Jackie
Kennedy's riding boots. Sight-seeing buses would follow
his limousine to his home in East Hampton where he
entertained Mlle. Matzabald's associates and bargain-
basement hippies. While he conducted the business of
the courtroom, his nose rested upon a purple satin pillow
Matzabald had made for him. This only added to his
difficulties. Ruthless art executives would try to swipe
the pillow so that they could exhibit it in their galleries.
Judge Whimplewopper asked the Screws to remove the
defendants' masks. They turned out to be M/Neighbor's
son and his little anarchist friend Joel O. I knew it.
I knew it. Their criticism of the state would get them
into trouble. I hoped the judge would be stern with
them and stern he was.

"You pair have been accused of trying to make it
across the Black Bay in a rowboat full of boxes of mouthwash. Whaddaya have to say for yourselves?"

"Well, your honor, all that I can say is that your
mama must have humped a whole bunch of anteaters
for you to have a snout like that. Which is to say more
for her than SAM's mother who gave a dying bull ele-
phant the clap," M/Neighbor's son replied.

Everybody in the courtroom got shook including me.

I only wished that the punishment issued would be severe.

"Now see here, you young punk, you can't talk about me and SAM's mothers like that. They've been dead for years, God rest their souls."

"Yes and they've probably given all the worms in the cemetery lockjaw by now," added Joel O.

"Thirty days for contempt of court!" the judge screamed, weeping profusely.

Suddenly a man ran down the aisle of the courtroom, swiped the pillow and dashed toward the side exit. "Come back here with that pillow! One of you Screws stop that man!" It was the president of the Yellow Cab Company. The man was captured and whisked off to a room near the courtroom. The Screws returned the pillow to the bench, lifting the judge's nose and gently placing the pillow underneath.

"Dat's more like it," the judge said, combing his pink bangs with a yard-long comb. His hair had been teased and fashioned at Mlle. Matzabald's Mudpie Factory. "Some of these art dealers ain't got no RUTH," the judge editorialized. "Now I'm going to give you 'linguints thirty days in the tombs for rapping about SAM's and my ol ladies and playing the dozens like that." An attorney for civil liberties rose to object to the arbitrary something or other. Seems that he didn't like the way Judge Whimplewopper was handling the insolent youngsters. Before he could continue the Screws had tackled him, and putting a full Nelson on the man hustled him from the courtroom.

"Object nothin'—this is my courtroom and I was duly appointed by the Dictator of HIMSELF and I don't 'low a bunch of willy-nilly nervous Nellie chumps to kick up no fuss. Right, boys?"

"Right!" answered the Screws, snapping to a position of parade rest.

"So you creeps want to get tough, huh? Another remark about my ma and I'll give you a contempt citation. We'll see about burn the baby burn. Now what have you to say for yourself?" Whimplewopper said, turning to the boy anarchist.

"We were going to take Sam's Island, kidnap the motherfuker and make him tell the truth about those fourteen people who were killed up there in the John last week. We were going to pour gallons of mouthwash in the sucker's mouth until he gave it to us straight," Joel O. explained.

"Well for your info, kiddo, I personally headed the commission what investigated that matter and there were pretty respectable fellas on it—including Mr. Nancy Spellman, Chief Nazarene Bishop and vicar of the Screws; Irving Gooseman, a well-known philanthropist and civic leader; Aboreal Hairyman, our roving ambassador; and a very nice colored gentleman who was a retired head of the colored Elks of the world. These are men with fine backgrounds and they don't be telling no fibs so I'm going to give you thirty more days for holding these men in contempt and impugning their reputations. And that goes for all those commie joos out there who were writing up all them books and articles about me and the fellas who sat on that distinguished commission. If I ever get you guys in my courtroom, I'll teach you commie scum a little trick. You know it was a rabbinical committee what wrote them articles what brought down the Roman Empire and I don't want that happening here. We won't stand for it."

"How did a handicapped mind like yours ever get into judicial robes anyway, you weird-looking little moxy? I bet your joint's the size of a flea."

"He may be tiny, Joel O., but he's a swinger," said M/Neighbor's son. "I saw him in *Time* magazine once with some really boss-looking broads. He seemed a little high and was showing them how to do the black bottom singing corny stuff like boo-boop-a-doop and wearing a fun hat on his nose." The two defendants cracked up and laughter resounded in the courtroom.

"But he must be a switch-hitter, baby, because he had to go downtown on SAM in order to get the job."

"Wait a minute! Whatta you think this is, some lousy social work clinic? Thirty years for arson, possession of illegal drugs and going from city to city to start riots! I'm fed up with you kids doing nigger dances and wearing your hair long. You seem to be having a lot of fun. Maybe thirty years in a federal prison will straighten you guys out. Take um away, Screws."

Joel O. spat on the nose.

"GETUM OUTTAHERE," he screamed as a Screw dutifully polished his snout.

"Fuk you and your generation of ghosts! We'll convert the prisoners! None of you ol crow eyes over sixty will stop our drive."

"Get rid of um, willya?" Whimplewopper ordered his Screws, as he gulped down a fistful of Miltown. "I'll surely wet the bed tonight. It was better in the fifties when I presided over the bird hearings. Everybody was polite and dignified. Used big words like quibbicale and didn't take no offense because I youse to be a hog caller. Those boys made me muss my pink bangs, sniff, sniff. There will be a ten-minute recess while I get myself together," the judge sobbed, as two Screws assisted him from the courtroom.

When the nose returned, my case was called by the clerk. "Fannie Mae Doopeyduk versus Bukka Doopeyduk. Will the parties please come fawwad," the court clerk said.

Fannie Mae wore a black slouchy hat and stood in high black heels and a black dress which made her seem hipless. Her eyes avoided mine as we stood side by side before Judge Whimplewopper.

"What seems to be the problem?" The lengthy bulbous nose peered at Fannie Mae.

"I tried to be a good wife, yo honnah," she began. "As my grandmother used to say, 'A hard head makes a soft ass,' so I told him to go to da Harry Sam Ear Muffle Factory where they was hirin' and where they makes some good change. But no. He wouldn't listen. Having a hard head he rather work in that hospital where they got all kinds of screwballs skipping around. We nevvah had 'nough money for the fun I likes to have and whenever my girl friends come over to the house to play whist, he was always rude. Then finally yo honnah, one day he tried to viscerate me!"

"Viscerate you?" the nose said.

"Yes, viscerate me." A chorus of aws and a few psts swept the courtroom. The nose turned to me.

"What do you have to say about visceratin'—I mean eviscerating your wife?"

I lowered my head and folding my hands in front of me answered. "Well your honor . . . I did . . . it . . . because I had become a . . . a . . . a . . . hoodooed."

Tumult in the courtroom. Reporters holding the top of
their hats rushed to telephone.

"Quiet, quiet!" the judge said. "Order in the court. Do
you expect me to believe such a thing?"

"It's true," I said to the nose with freckles on the tip.
"My professor, U2 Polyglot, was rolling a ball about
Europe on his hands and knees and cured me after I
galloped into him. This was about the time the Chinese
drove into the suburbs on bicycles with skulls for handle-
bars and kidnaped those heel-kicking housewives hanging
out the wash. Well, to make a long story short, the
professor had gotten this bottle of de-hoodoo lotion from
my wife's grandmother who is an ol witch taking conjure lessons through the mail under the Mojo Power
Retraining Act. You see, she looks after her son who
sits about the house all day in antlers. Well, anyway,
the professor transformed me into my normal self and
I've been working very hard at the hospital where Nurse
Rosemary D Camp put me in charge of an ol man
who died kissing Versailles 1919, so now I have a lot
of time to devote to the movement whose leader has
been in the John for thirty years due to a weird malignant
illness. You see, we want him to get up off his big
fat—"

"Wait a minute, Hoooooollllllllllllllldddddddddittttt hoooo-
llllllllllldddddddddittttttttt," the judge said, turning his head
to the ceiling, making visible two dark nostrils and a
quivering red tonsil. "What's all this talk about an old
woman who pushes a ball around the world and a nurse
who sits in the john all day? Do you expect me to believe that?"

"With all due respect, your honor, you got it all wrong.
It's Dr. Christian who pushes the ball all day through

areas where nuns are raping the huns and my father-in-law kisses Versailles 1919. . . . I mean," fumbling and stammering. "No, it goes this way . . . a . . . a . . ."

But seeing my confusion a man in the audience sprang from his seat and stepping on the toes of his neighbors, rushed into the aisle. "You left out the ol woman who kidnaped Checkers."

And almost as swiftly another woman stood up and shouted, cupping her mouth with her hands, "Not to mention the plumbers' mutiny."

But the nose, resting on the bench like a stout lizard, interrupted the spectators. "Now look here, do you think I'm some kinda dunce? I mean, if SAM has taken Checkers, then who is in the John?"

Another man hopped to his feet and said, "Hey, yo honnah, that's catchy." He then went into the aisle and started a chant. "If SAM has kidnaped Checkers, then who is in the John?" He snapped his fingers and began the old a-one, a-two, a-three, kick. The courtroom audience joined, clapping on the beat. Another woman stood behind him and put her hands on his waist. Together they began a conga line. Soon the whole courtroom was in a conga line singing the ditty, "If SAM has kidnapped Checkers, then who is in the John? A-one, a-two, a-three, kick." Suddenly the doors of the courtroom flew open and an orchestra of men in damp white dinner jackets rushed in. Their hair was dripping wet and fish flew from their pockets. The musicians accompanied the spectators, putting their soggy violin bows to strings and playing marimbas and steel drums.

I went apeshit. "WHAT DO YOU THINK THIS IS, SOME KINDA JOKE OR SUMTHIN? STOP THIS MONKEY BUSINESS RIGHT NOW! YOU KNOW THIS

PLACE IS NOWHERE. NOTHIN' BUT A BIG KLANG-
A-LANG-A-DING-DONG-A-RAZZ-A-MA-TAZ."

The judge jumped up and waving his arms cried,
"STOP IT! STOP IT!" He took out a whistle, puffed
his jaws and blew. "DO YOU THINK AMERICAN
JUSTICE IS SOME KINDA WEIRD CIRCUS? SOME
FREAKISH SIDE SHOW? A CARNIVAL ROUTINE?"
Everybody hurried back to their seats and the orchestra
rushed from the courtroom.

"Now that's more like it," the nose said. "We will
continue with the case." The nose turned to me and
with its beady eyes piercing through the wig said, "I'm
not going to have my circus . . . turned into a courtroom . . . dog bite it." He combed his bangs again. "I
mean I'm not going to have my courtroom turned into
a circus, unnerstand? It's clear to me, Mr. Doopeyduk,
that you are a disagreeable person whose head is always
in the clouds. Imagine such ravings. If I didn't know
that you were a Nazarene apprentice, I'd think you were
off your rocker."

"He talks like dat all the time, yo honnah," Fannie
Mae added, putting her two cents in, tapping her foot
and looking at me evilly. "Always talkin' all out his
head."

I looked up to the nose and said, "I'm sorry for turning
your courtroom into a circus, your honor. I'll take whatever's coming to me."

"Very well, then," the nose said. "I award your wife
a separation and fifty per cent of your salary will go
to her for support." With this he banged his gavel and
called for the next case. I turned around to leave, almost
bumping into the next case which was the bearded lady
and the fat woman who had brought the juggler into

court for hitting them over the head with the lion tamer's stool. I walked down the steps of the courtroom just as the limousine with antlers sticking from the roof pulled away from the curb.

PART IV

Loopholes and Hoopla Hoops

The next morning I was fired from my job. When I opened the door of the floor the orderlies were waiting for me. "Mrs. Nurse Rosemary D Camp wants to see you, Doopeyduk."

I went into Mrs. Nurse Rosemary D Camp's office. Standing next to her in a gray double-breasted business suit with a stethoscope hanging around his neck was Dr. Christian. "Mr. Doopeyduk," Mrs. D Camp began, "I can't begin to tell you how sorry I am about the action the hospital is going to take against you so I brought down Dr. Christian to explain to you why we deem it necessary to let you go at this time."

"Let me go," I said. "I don't understand."

"You tell him, please, Dr. Christian, please," Rosemary D Camp said.

He walked over to me and put his hand on my

shoulder. "Yes, my boy," he said, shaking his head, "we were all prepared to give you a job in the surgical department where you would be in charge of the other nurses' aides and orderlies who clean up leftovers from the operations. But you see, Bukka, it's hard for us to keep on people who have outside financial trouble."

"Outside financial trouble?"

"Yes. Show him the order," he said, turning to the nurse. It was the greenish-brown seal from the court ordering the hospital to deduct 50 per cent of my salary each week.

"Yes, you see, Mr. Doopeyduk," the doctor said, his back turned to me as he looked out of the window, "we can't afford the clerical help necessary to take care of garnisheed wages. We are a nonprofit institution here to service mankind, the Hippocratic oath and all that," he said, removing his glasses and pinching the bridge of his nose. "I'm afraid we're going to have to take back your golden bedpan."

I dropped to my knees and threw the kat all kinds of Al Jolson mammies one after the other, but he wasn't impressed. "O, don't," I cried, tugging at his pants. "Don't take the golden bedpan, don't take it, do anything but don't take the golden bedpan."

A sparkling tear of rainbow colors appeared in Nurse Rosemary D Camp's eye and rolled down her plump pink cheek. "Don't worry, my boy," Dr. Christian said. "I'm sure we will hear great things from you. You shouldn't have any trouble at all, you look just like Sidney Poitier, Jackie Robinson, Nat King Cole, Joe Louis, Harry Belafonte, and Ralph Bunche, so, no sweat. Good-bye, Bukka, here is three weeks' salary," he said, giving me a small envelope.

I walked down the steps of the hospital. It had begun to rain. Here I was, I thought, twenty-three years old. Lost a job and lost a wife. The future looked quite dim. I drew up my collar and walked through the streets to the sound of the foghorn coming from the pier. I reached into my pocket for a smoke. I felt a card. It was a pink card given to me by the ol man in the Seventeen Nation Disarmament Conference Bar. It was wrinkled and moist. It said, "Go to Entropy Productions. Collect 200 dollars." Things were looking up. A cloud moved above sagging with rain. It seemed as if it had eyes, nose, lips. It did, my eyes, nose, and lips. Get it. Clouds. Head in the clouds.

Entropy Productions was located in the Lower East Side of this WAY OUT BRING DOWN, this sifting area of BAD NEWS, this ugly TRIPS FESTIVAL. Its manager was Cipher X who graduated from M.I.T. in mechanical drawing—but having abandoned this career, he lived in a loft where he made big black gorgeous hoopla hoops with his own wittle hands.

Well, not exactly. Cipher, which means zero, would make a sketch including his specifications and send it off to GENERAL DYNAMICS CORPORATION which in turn would send him a brand new hoopla hoop every two weeks. Cipher was the darling of the fire insurance underwriters, airline ticket reservation clerks, female book editors from Skidmore and the wives of these groups who would flock to the loft to witness his *BECOMINGS*, as they were called. The loft was situated in a run-down factory on Oriental Avenue.

I had moved from the projects that morning because of that rule which forbade single people to live in them.

I was broke, having spent three weeks' salary on some
rare Nazarene books so as to better prepare myself for
a deep thoroughgoing scrutiny of the faith. I must have
seemed a little bedraggled as I walked along the street
with the bag containing my belongings. The bag was
tied to a stick and I carried it over my shoulder.

The door said: ENTROPY PRODUCTIONS: FLOAT
IN. I opened the door and was tackled by a slim, agile
man who wore tight-fitting black pants and a black T-
shirt. His feet were bare. Sitting on my chest he began
to measure my neck and wrists with a tape.

"You'll do," said the angular nose, the thin lips, the
sterling high cheekbones.

"I'll do? I'll do for what?" I asked, sitting up.

"You'll do for my great BECOMING 'Git It On.'"

"But I don't understand," I pleaded. "The man over
at the Seventeen Nation Disarmament Bar didn't say anything about a theatrical production."

"Theater? Acting?" He frowned. "Those old men over
there are just a bunch of losers talking nothing but a
lot of dumb cannon fire and the way things used to
be. Their notion of the world went out with the pro-
scenium arch.

"All things are theater," he said, vaulting to his feet
and wildly gesticulating. "A child playing with a beach
ball, a bus driver taking a token instead of twenty
cents. Why when I attend a concert, I'm more interested
in the spit that leaks from the horn valves than the
music. O, I can go on and on. Why every time I hear a
newborn baby cry or touch a leaf or—"

"But how do you know I'll do well in this BECOM-
ING?" I said, cutting him off.

"You," he said, holding my chin, "are a natural. That face, the face of a sphinx, your ample neck, those lean, hard wrists. Tomorrow night's BECOMING should be a stirring one."

"Tomorrow night? But aren't we supposed to have an audition or a rehearsal?"

"Idiot!" he sneered. "Auditions? Rehearsals? There you go again talking like the Seventeen Nation Disarmament Conference Bar. Why don't you do as you're told. Just show tomorrow night at eight thirty and we'll just allow things to drift. Now no more of these questions," he said, putting twenty ten-dollar bills into my hand.

"Why, I can't take this. I haven't done an honest day's work. Right here in the Nazarene manual," I continued, removing my trusty little booklet from a pocket. "Allow me to quote from our beloved Bishop Nancy Spellman: 'One must sweat one's balls off to be *a head* in SAM's.' "

But Cipher X had crossed to the other side of the room and was now kneeling before the big black hoopla hoop which hung from the wall by a nail. Not wishing to interrupt the man's meditations, I went out of the building and walked toward Connecticut Avenue.

I came upon a room-for-rent sign displayed in the window of a tenement building. I rang the super's bell. A nattily dressed bearded man wearing a fez opened the door. It was my friend Elijah Raven, the heretic Nazarene apprentice.

"Bukka Doopeyduk, you ol son of a gun. What are you doing here?"

"Elijah, my good man," I answered his greeting as we warmly embraced. "You were saying 'Flim Flam

Alakazam' last time we saw each other. Aren't you still
with the Jackal-headed Front?"

"No good, baby. It all turned out to be a plot. What a
hummer that was, man. Made me real disillusioned and
cynical about organizations. You see, the CIA controlled
the organization through an ol geezer who was given to
such eccentricities as wearing cobwebbed antlers all the
time. In fact, the kat was eating pork on the side and had
a Betty Grable pinup on his wall; and to make things
worse, his mother, I mean the man's own mother, put the
hoodoo not only on the people in the ghetto but one-
third of the planet. They made themselves rich by getting
the patent on a solution that would de-hoodoo people
they'd put the hoodoo on. Well, just as we uncovered
that the mystery man behind the organization was this
joker, SAM made him ambassador to Luxembourg. Man,
we got our nickel plates and were heading for the pier
to ice the kat. But just as we drove up to the dock the
Queen Mary was pulling away and the cocksucker was
sticking his tongue out and laughing at us. And you
should have seen the party they had. Governesses, maids,
companions, manicurists, domestics and a beautiful fly
black chick. Man, all kinds of o-fay kats were on their
knees in their tuxedos and tall hats serenading her like
in those 1930 musicals. She was decked out from head to
foot in some of those chic saber-toothed fashions for ag-
gressive living."

"I wonder, did they take the antler polish?" I pondered
out loud.

"What was that, Bukka?"

"Never mind, Elijah, you'd never believe it."

"As I was saying, Bukka, the Queen Mary pulled off
with this really Hanging-Gardens-of-Babylon scene tak-

ing place on the deck and this traitor that the CIA had picked was surrounded by all of these old blue gums holding ear trumpets and shaking hands with some hooting crackers in creme-colored ten-gallon hats. Man, I was really down in the dumps after that but now I've recovered. I moved down here to write plays about 'Git It On.'"

"'Git It On'?" I cried. "Why that's the same thing I'm preparing for. Cipher X, the white BECOMINGS king, and I are doing a thing called 'Git It On.'"

"Cipher X," Elijah scowled. "Man, watch that kat. Whitey is a born devil. Snakes hide in his tongue muscles."

"O, I don't know, Elijah. Cipher seems to be pretty serious. He's in his loft all day fashioning those hoopla hoops. Why, some of them hang in the American collection at the Metropolitan. He even gave me a two-hundred-dollar advance and I haven't performed yet. Now if you'll excuse me, Elijah, I'd like to find the super so that I can inquire about the room for rent."

"The super," he said, breathing on his knuckles and rubbing them up and down his chest. "You're looking at the super, my man. I'm the agent in this house. You see, I collect rent for a kat named Irving Gooseman and the dwarf assistant Slickhead Fopnick he got from the Urban League. Two characters the likes of which you'll never see. Once a month they come pouring in here, all out of breath and waving a rod. A real heat. Man, those kats are always in a hurry. Then they put the money in a sack and they're gone, quick as a flash. You should see them speeding around the corner at one hundred miles an hour in that T-Model looking as if they'd seen a ghost. And the kids and dogs and people on the street are like climbing trees and leaping into the air trying to get out of their way.

"Anyway, I'm just the agent, kinda like a catalyst. Little does the Joo know that I'm secretly collecting milk bottles and rags as I prepare for 'Git It On' right under my man's nose. See, I'm a poet down here in this artistic community, going around saying mothafuka in public by night, but by day I'm stacking milk bottles in the closet instead of taking them back to the store for the two cents deposit. That's what you might call out-maneuvering whitey."

"There's no two-cent deposit on milk bottles these days, and they're disposable," I said.

"There isn't? Well, that's even better because Borden's and Sealtest won't even miss them. Hey, Bukka, you're smart. Why don't you help me and the brothers work on a manual for urban guerrilla warfare?"

"I'm too busy looking for loopholes in the Nazarene manual."

"Bukka, don't you know that HARRY SAM has body odor?"

Another one, I thought, but too weary to take up the challenge, I said, "If you don't mind, Elijah, I'm kinda tired. Would you mind showing me the room?" I followed him up the stairs.

"By the way," he said, looking over his shoulder, "is Fannie Mae moving down here?"

"No," I answered. "You see about the time Art Link-letter awarded a life supply of pigeons to these . . . I mean . . . you see, I became hoodooed and the China-men slashed Dr. Christian . . . just let's say we broke up, Elijah."

"Sorry to hear that, Bukka," he said, turning the key in the lock.

A large sink, a chest of drawers and a closet. Atop the chest was a basin of water and a towel. There were also some Hershey-bar wrappers.

"O, Bukka," he said, picking up the wrappers, "the last tenant here was a transient who rented for two days. She was a former movie star and the chick was so tired that she slept the entire time. That'll be ten bucks a week, Bukka. Pay promptly on Friday."

"It's a deal," I said, untying my bag on the top of the chest.

"See you later, my man," Elijah said, closing the door of the room behind him. I placed the spittoon next to the bed, the remaining Picayunes I put in my coat pocket, washed out some shorts with the gold dust twins then went to the sink and put the elbow baking soda in a glass of water. After drinking it down I looked at the gold pocket watch: it was July 5, 1945. I fell back on the bed and got a long shot of shut-eye.

I spent the next day lying in bed and reading the Nazarene manual for loopholes and making notes in the margins. There were certain things about the doctrine that confused me. For example, the Nazarene apocalypse. What sort of commode should HARRY SAM be sitting upon? Should it be a pink plastic one or one made of mahogany? Should it be done in lavender with a beautiful ring of fur on the seat? I didn't even want to get into the subject of tissue; that one stumped the best scholars in the movement. What about the sanitary, safe modern breeze style? This notion would certainly get me into difficulty with the conservative wing. Some of *them* still preferred the outhouse with the half-moon window. And others were so reactionary that they fought and broke chairs on one another's heads at conventions over the issue of the squat method or as the kats on the block used to say, "wherever you be let your water run free." I certainly couldn't use dialect, as it was called. The academicians would circulate a petition:

> *We refuse to sit back on our RANDS and listen to the steady erosion of the English language. Not since Caxton has there been such a crisis in letters. For many years now we've been lecturing on how Dostoyevsky ate cabbages and have tolerated (giving themselves away) the ADULTERATION of HER TONGUE. Now we feel it's time to speak out. There will be a twilight vigil at the grave site of RUTHERFORD BIRCHARD HAYES in Spiegel Grove State Park, Fremont, Ohio. All those who feel as we do please try to be present. Buses will leave at 6:00 a.m. A potluck lunch will be prepared by the Assistant Dean of Arts and Sciences from the University of Buffalo. Then a community sing will be led by BENNETT CERF and BERGEN EVANS.*

So you see these were thorny and profound questions not to be taken lightly. I would have to study and study hard.

The time had arrived for the performance. In line were the interior decorators, male nurses from the University of Rochester and the entire student body and faculty of the University of Buffalo holding surfboards, plus the mayor of that great city. Stephen Wolinski was dressed in black-and-white-checkered bow tie, a chartreuse cap, patent leather shoes, and trousers known in the forties as "cootie drapes." The Society of Mechanical Drawers was also present and they brought along the wives of all these groups who had been posing for underground films all day. Is that all? No, wait! Hundreds of yellow cabs pull up in front of the building. It is the head of the Yellow Cab Company, a true patron of the arts, followed by his entire fleet who remove their caps in respect for KULCHUR.

Inside the loft the people sat on newspapers which were laid about the floor. A movie projector stood in the aisle. I went into Cipher's office.

"Well, Bukka," he said, doing the hoopla hoop. "Do you feel nervous?"

"Just a little, Cipher meaning Zero," I said. "Where do I change into my costume?"

He slapped his hand against his forehead as the hoopla hoop slipped down around his thighs. "Can't you learn? Look," he said, opening the door of the office. "See that stock over there before the front row of audience?" He pointed to a stock—the kind used for punishment in the American colonies. Behind the stock and mounted on a table was a tape recorder. Standing next to the table was a roll-out movie screen. "Just go there and put your neck and wrists in that stock, there's a pillow behind it that you can rest your knees upon. Put this gag on." He tied a piece of cloth over my mouth, then turned me around so that I faced the stock.

It seemed simple enough so I walked out stepping over the people in the audience as I made my way toward the stock. There was scattered applause. I put my neck and hands through the stock and knelt on the pillow. The stock clamped shut. I looked worriedly at Cipher who only stood in the door of the office with his arms folded and his legs apart. He was immobile in his dark glasses. I tried to wriggle out of the stock making muffled cries through the gag for help. A movie projector showed athletes jumping over hurdles at the 1936 German Olympics. The audience didn't seem to hear me. They were busily exchanging cogent comments.

"Do you think it's Christ hanging off the cross?" whispered a businessman who had made a fortune in pot holders.

"No, I was reading Jessie Weston the other day and it's all about yams," replied a hairdresser from the East Bronx.

The door of the loft swung open. And the taxi dancers from the BUCK-RABBIT CLUB and their aviation executive escorts moved to one side as a robot with stroboscopic lights for eyes moved around the loft. The newspapers rustled while on the screen the Hitlerjugend marched past the dictator, proudly displaying flags. Finally after rolling about the floor the robot stood before me. It opened a panel in its chest and removed a baseball. It then threw the baseball into my face. In rapid succession it removed baseballs and threw them at me and red lumps began to rise on my face. I looked, eyes imploringly, to Cipher X for relief but he simply stood quietly in the door inspecting the stock, screen and robot. The tape recorder switched on.

WHITEY YOU DIE TOMORROW RIGHT AFTER BREAKFAST AND IF YOU DON'T DIE THEN CHOKING ON YOUR WAFFLES DON'T BREATHE A SIGH OF RELIEF AND SAY THANK GOD FOR BUFFERIN 'CAUSE THAT WILL ONLY MEAN THAT YOU WILL MEET YOUR MAKER COME THE VERY NEXT DAY. HEAH THAT. HEAH THAT, WHITEY, ON THE NEXT SUNNY DAY YOU WILL MEET YOUR DEMISE, YOU BEASTS CREATURES OF THE DEEP. 'CAUSE YOU CAN'T HOLD UP A CANDLE TO US VIRILE BLACK PEOPLE. LOOK AT THAT MUSCLE. COME ON UP HERE CHARLIE

AND FEEL THAT MUSCLE. IF YOU DON'T WATCH OUT WE WILL
BREAK INTO THOM MCAN'S TOMORROW AND STEAL ALL THE
SHOES. HEAH THAT, ANIMALS. TOMORROW NIGHT AT FIFTY-
NINE SECONDS PAST EIGHT EVERY LAST PAIR OF MOCCASINS
WILL BE GONE. COME ON, STEP ACROSS THAT LINE. STEP
ACROSS THAT LINE AND KNOCK OFF THAT CHIP. . . .

The robot swallowed the baseballs on the floor and
quickly exited. The clamps snapped away from my neck
and hands. The projector was turned off. Cipher X
ran from the office door to the stock to thunderous applause. I could not believe it, the audience was applaud-
ing its own doom. I gazed out through my puffy eyelids,
as the audience stood on its feet cheering us. Cipher
lifted me from the stock and hand in hand we bowed to
the audience from side to side. A man crawling on his
hands and knees slid up to me followed by a pack of reporters. He dropped his pad from his teeth and with a
pencil between his toes began to ask me questions.

He was J. Lapp Swine, jazz critic from the *Deformed
Demokrat*. He tugged my pants cuffs and asked, "How
does it feel to have all that rhythm, Mr. Doopeyduk?
Tell me, huh? Won'tcha please? Won'tcha?"

Cipher X threw up his hands and said, "Be patient,
fellows. I'll answer all your questions in my news conference." He took me by the elbows—the fuken elbow
grabber with sterling high cheekbones—and escorted me
through the throng of well-wishers toward his office. We
had difficulty getting through. The Assistant Dean of
Arts and Sciences from the University of Buffalo with a
surfboard tied to his back and a long petition hanging
from his hands accosted us.

"Mr. Doopeybuk and Cipher X," he said, his wife on
his arm. "We're just crazy about BECOMINGS and

HOOPLA HOOPS and LOOPHOLES. Why just last week my wife and I rushed to the A&P and bought nineteen of those big black beauties. And just because we're way up there in Buffalo which is eighty per cent Polish-American doesn't mean that we don't keep up with what's happening in NOWHERE. Why, we read the *Deformed Demokrat* each week, religiously."

Cipher shoved the man aside and continued toward the office. "Sir, Mr. Doopeyduk and I have to go into my office to relax. The performance was truly exhausting," Cipher lisped.

But the man kept talking. "We just thought that you might want to sign this petition concerning the erosion and bastardization of the tongue!"

"I'm sorry, sir," Cipher answered, fluttering his eyelids. "I'm neutral in all things. Besides I have a very nice soft and juicy tongue, so there," Cipher said, sticking out his tongue at the man and continuing toward the office.

The man and his wife went back to the mayor, Stephen Wolinski, who standing in the corner asked, "Did he say anything about da snowplows and da bombed-out swimming pools?"

Inside the office Cipher pulled the gag off my mouth and then I BLEW MY COOL.

"WHADDAYA MEAN PUTTIN' ME UP THERE WITH THEM BASEBALLS KNOCKING ME FACE-LESS AND THEM CRAZY SPEECHES AND STUFF? YOU TRYIN' TO GET ME BUMPED OFF OR SOME-THIN'? WHY I GOT A GOOD MIND TO HIT YOU RIGHT SMACK IN THE KISSER!"

"Cutey poo," he said, prancing about the office, the tips of his left and right hands touching. "Sweetheart.

Dearest. I'm completely pooped from the BECOMING! You were so absolutely adorable," he said, "come here. Let me puck you one on the cheek. Let me grease your palm," he said, applying some Vaseline to my palm which had been bruised. As a Nazarene apprentice I was completely disarmed in the face of such kindness.

"ALL RIGHT, BUT YOU'D BETTER COME UP WITH SOMETHIN' GOOD, BUDDY."

"Do come back tomorrow and we'll discuss the BE-COMING," he said.

"All right. I yield to art this time, but tomorrow I want a full-dress review of this thing."

I walked down the steps into the streets. Just as I stepped into the area in front of the loft, someone whispered from the shadows. "Pssssssssssst, Bukka Doopeyduk, Bukka Doopeyduk. Come over here."

I walked over to the figure standing in the corner.

"Look, Bukka," the figure said. "Dose people over there told me dat you knew where I could get some snowplows and some cement. See dim Chinamens came into Williamsville and Snyder last week and bombed out all da swimmin' pools?"

"I'm sorry, Jim. I can't help you," I told the mayor of Buffalo, Stephen Wolinski. "I know that it is an inconvenience and all, but I got troubles of my own."

I left the mayor of Buffalo looking like a sad sack as he walked holding out the insides of his pockets toward the student and faculty delegation who stood next to sightseeing buses looking disappointed. I was surrounded by fans holding autograph pads. BECOMINGS' followers were standing deep in front of the buildings discussing the performance. Ratner's was filled to capacity.

The next morning I ran out of the house and returned
with an armful of newspapers. I nearly fainted dead
away when I read the headlines in *the ny teeth.*

ACTOR CALLS FOR GUERRILLA WARFARE AGAINST SAM.
CALLS DICTATOR A BARN BURNER.
POPE GIVES UP AS BINGO CRISIS ESCALATES. TAKE THE GOD-
DAMNED CARDS, WEARY PONTIFF SAYS.
CHINESE ESCAPE THROUGH DUMBWAITER.
M/NEIGHBOR AND NOSETROUBLE DEMAND PARLEY ON MISS-
ING TOTS.

I put on my shoes and rushed downstairs to the telephone. I would have to call *the ny teeth* and get an ex-
traction. But before I could pick up the receiver, the
phone rang.

"Mr. Doopeyduk," a voice said. "This is Allen Hangup.
I'm emceeing the controversial new *Allen Hangup Show.*
We are going to have a discussion on how the migration
of the eastern brown pelican affects the civil rights movement."

"Man, I don't know nothing about no birds," I told
the kat.

"That's fine," he said. "Tweet, tweet, see you soon."
(Click.)

The phone rang again. "Hello, Mr. Doopeyduk," another voice said. "This is *Poison Dart* magazine, the
magazine of black liberation. We are having a symposium
on the role of the black writer in contemporary society.
We will be covering such issues as: Should he glare at
Charlie? Should he kinda stick out his lower lip and look
mean? or should he just snag at Charlie's pants legs
until his mouth is full of ankles and calves and he gets

the sweet taste of Max Factor on his tongue? We shall also be discussing whether the brothers should part their hair on the side or part it down the middle. These are grave issues and you as a friend of the liberation movement shouldn't want to miss the discussion."

"Look," I answered. "I'm not an actor. I'm more of a clown."

"Good, Mr. Doopeyduk," the voice said. "So are we, tweet, tweet. See you soon."

This thing was getting all out of hand. I would have to go to the only man who was capable of setting the matter straight: CIPHER X. I ran out of the house and up the stairs of the factory building and pounded on the door. Cipher peeked out, followed by heavy clouds of smoke.

"Look, Bukka, I'll see you at the performance tonight. Right now I'm having a press conference, sweetheart." But before I could answer, the door was slammed in my face. I rushed to the corner and bought the afternoon paper *the ny whine*.

BUKKA DOOPEYDUK HAS EVERY RIGHT TO KILL, CIPHER X SAYS. JACKIE COUGHS. BOBBY HAS HICCUPS. TEDDY OPENS TOYTALK FAIR.

read growing up in soulsville first of three installments
—or what it means to be a backstage darky
by Cipher (o)

I ran back to the loft. Press conference or no press conference, this kat wasn't going to get me killed. This time I was trampled by reporters who flew down the steps and out of the loft to file their stories. (Man, I have to tell you that little J. Lapp Swine was keeping right up with them, galloping along like a jet-propelled groundhog.) I rushed into the office where Cipher X was pounding away at the typewriter.

"What's the matter, my man? Can't you see I'm writing this jazz review for *Buck* magazine?"

"Fuk *Buk* magazine," I said, jabbing my finger into the very pulp of *the ny whine*. "Are you trying to get me killed? You said that all a BECOMING was was a fusion of light, sound and film, always expanding, never complete. What are you telling the reporters these lies for? I have a good mind to punch you out, you fuken maypolegrabber with a skinny neck."

"Relax, my man, relax. I thought that you were hip. That you were into somethin'. But you're turning out to be as lame as all the others. Those headlines bring in the bread, my man. We couldn't eat without those headlines. Look at this," he said, pulling a wad of dough from the desk drawer big enough to choke a horse. "Why man, these rich kats are coming down here busting their nuts over you."

"But I'm not interested in fame or fortune. I just want to correct certain loopholes in the Nazarene manual. Sort of fortify the faith, so to speak."

"Well, man, you're interested in loopholes. I'm interested in hoopla hoops. I can't see why we can't collaborate—they both have diphthongs. This morning those diphthongs brought me twenty-five grand from some top government officials."

"GOVERNMENT OFFICIALS?" I said, tearing to the window and looking to the street below for suspicious-looking cars.

"What's your worry, my man?" Cipher X said. "They were in here all morning hopping around my er . . .

er . . . maypole in the nude. They paid me twenty-five grand for twenty hoopla hoops."

"Government officials?" I asked again, astonished. "What government officials?"

"Why, those kats across the Black Bay at the motel. They were up here this morning posing for some of my underground films. Didn't you hear them panting in the rear of the audience last night? Why, they all thought you were raw and powerful. And 'a little cute too' as one of the high officials put it."

"But didn't they get upset at all the invective from that tape recorder? And what about the news stories?"

"Aw man, you got them kats all wrong. Why, they're real swingers. You should see them up there getting away. Why, they stomp up a storm."

"YOU'VE BEEN TO THE HARRY SAM MOTEL?" I asked.

"Sure, baby, they're my best customers. Why, I just go up there and ring the bell like a little old Avon lady and stone take care of business. I mean, those kats are not like the creeps around here: eating a whole lot of dumb brown rice and taking up collections for a gallon of Paisano wine or kneeling and worshiping some big fat lazy gook. They are really TOGETHER. I mean, it's a groovy nowhere, if you know how."

I felt better.

"Here," Cipher said, giving me a slim ruffled cigarette. "The kids up at Walden High School smoke these. Take a drag."

I felt much better. "Well, Cipher, do you really think that I can make a career at BECOMINGS and study loopholes too?"

"Sure, baby," Cipher answered. "Why, the art crowd is crazy about you. Look at what this kat in the *Deformed Demokrat* says:

AFTER BEING STUMPED BY CECIL TAYLOR AND ARCHIE SHEPP IT DID THIS CRIPPLED MIND SOME GOOD TO SEE OL BONES

"He said that about me?" I asked, pleased.

"Sure, my man, you're on your way to big things. Now let me get back to my article before the typewriter gets lockjaw and gum in the keys."

I walked out of the loft possessed. A BECOMINGS person. I was really on the way now. I went into a store and bought a cigarette holder, a beret and some shades. Then I went into the drugstore and purchased Band-Aids, gauze and iodine. I decided to buy *Buck* magazine to read one of Cipher's jazz articles before going to bed. I settled back and leafed through the pages until I saw Cipher's by-line:

HOW TO BE A HIP KITTY AND A COOL COOL DADDY O

The next month went by rapidly with Cipher and me playing to standing-room-only crowds in the Hamptons, Provincetown, Woodstock, and Fremont, Ohio. I was invited to make personal appearances on radio and television; but soon it became known—after an interview in the *Deformed Demokrat*—that I was a loner, preferring to remain near the midnight oil—as it were—shirt-sleeved and diligently poring over Nazarene volumes. After this they stopped pestering me.

All the hippy bishops from the Church of Christ's Disciples sent me fan mail; some even went so far as to send me the rattlesnake leavings from their altars.

My name appeared in the newspapers each day:

DOOPEYDUK WARNS: FROGS, BOILS, LOCUSTS, FIRE, GLACIERS, ASTEROIDS.

One day I received a small linen cloth envelope. I enacted somersaults over its contents,

YOU ARE INVITED TO A BAD TRIP
AT THE HARRY SAM MOTEL. MUSIC BY CHET BAKER
FUN, STROBOSCOPIC LIGHTS, HOOPLA HOOPS AND
FRANK PRANKS (SMILE)
a driver will call for you at 12:00 A.M.
August 6th, 1945

I looked at my gold pocket watch. (That was tomorrow night.)

Just as I started up the steps the telephone rang. On the other end a voice exclaimed, "Mr. Doopeyduk, this is the *Allen Hangup Show* again. We would like to interview you tonight on the subject of 'Git It On.'"

"Look, my man" (going colored on the kat), "I cannot be participating in no show. I thought you fellows knew that I'm studying the Nazarene faith in my spare time. Why, just the other day Nancy Spellman and I were discussing game theory. The Bishop seemed quite worried."

"Mr. Doopeyduk," the voice said. "I neglected to say that Cipher and I are good friends and I thought—seeing as how he's done you so many favors—you might do it as a favor to him. He and I run a head shop out on Fire Island. We give up strange recipes to people."

"I'll make an exception this time," I said. "As a favor to Cipher, but in the future you won't be successful enlisting me for the show."

"O, WONDERFUL, Mr. Doopeyduk," the voice answered. "See you tonight."

We sat on a sofa behind a table with a tea service on the top. Allen Hangup had his blond hair done at Mlle. Pandy Matzabald's Mudpie Salon. Little pockets of flesh hung underneath his eyelids. He was a middle-aged medium-height man wearing a mod tie. A man stood before us holding a card which was the signal for the show to begin. It was one of those informal programs in which the viewer could even witness the cameras wheeling in and out of the studio, bare except for a round platform supporting the sofa and table.

"Ladies and gentlemen," Hangup began. "Our guest tonight is none other than the star of the Broadway-three-offs-removed hit, 'Git It On.' 'Git It On' has become such a box-office success that it's being considered for the Lincoln Center for Performing Arts."

It wasn't warm in the studio, but nevertheless Hangup began removing his tie and moving a finger around his wet collar.

"It's been unanimously acclaimed by the trustees of the Eugene Saxton Foundation and such magazines as *Good Housekeeping*. If you haven't seen 'Git It On' before, see it now. It's in its fourth week," he started to say but then sticking his tongue over the side of his lip and panting, he lunged for my throat and throwing his papers to the floor shouted, "OKAY DOOPEYDUK, TELL US WHEN WE GONE GIT IT ON."

"MAN, WILL SOMEBODY GET THIS KAT OFF ME?" I yelled. The man in the control room bolted through its door and came to my assistance, giving him a cup of Miltown and water. A commercial was substituted.

"DO YOU HAVE A CHINAMAN IN YOUR DUMB-WAITER?"

When Allen Hangup was perfectly calm a man holding an earphone and bending on one knee reprimanded the moderator. "Hangup, we warned you about this. If you continue to break down each time 'Git It On' is the topic for the Allen Hangup Show, we'll just have to call upstairs and see if J.C. can't get somebody else for the gig."

"I know. I know," said Hangup, shaking his head sadly and turning to me. "I'm really sorry, Mr. Doopeyduk. It's just that they've had twelve moderators before me who had the same problem. They expect you to be a passionless machine like those cameras over there. But I'm not a stone, an empty shell; I'm human and I get damp in the crotch like all the others (sigh) when 'Git It On' is discussed."

"I can forgive passion," I answered, "but the next time watch the vines, my man. They're expensive," I said, tidying my mussed suit.

"Just be careful," the engineer said to Hangup and returned to the studio.

The commercial was concluding—"THEN TAKE DAT GOOK BY THE NECK AND SLAM DAT GOOK. . . ."

The show continued.

"Mr. Doopeyduk," the composed Hangup said, "what do you think about this grand place?"

"Grand? Are you for real? You call this FAR OUT grand? Why, the only issue is whether those kats up there in the watercloset (FCC rules were stringent) will get off their big fat rumps and come out."

"Mr. Doopeyduk," Hangup continued, "why I haven't heard such vile language about the land we all love since my years in radio. Such demagogic things to say about this country."

"Land! Country! Man, those people have been up there in that foul nasty place for thirty years dripping feces everywhere they prowl and you got the nerve to talk about land and country. Are you off the wall?"

"Mr. Doopeyduk, this is the bastion of liberty and democracy, the citadel of fair play, the bulwark of individual liberty."

"Aw man, cut out the stone walls. Why, anybody in his right mind knows that this is a BIG WAY-OUT BRINGDOWN," I said, my voice rising. "There are things going on in HARRY SAM that will give you the willies. It bothers me 'cause I loves HIMSELF so much. Bats fly into his stomach walls and shit in his brain. And there's horrible screaming inside as funny lookin' monsters tramp through his testicles searching for food. Enchanted areas where the undead travel around on motorized golf carts. Why, I can go on for days. A bunch of ol people singing 'Roger Young' off-key, forgetting the words and trying to unload Hadrian's rock on suckers. A collection of rusty trumpets and a wheelbarrow full of heroic couplets and fugues. Who in his right mind would want to buy a rock or a wheelbarrow full of dead verse? Why, just the other day I saw a man running out of a bar yelling: 'Just like Munich, just like Munich.' WHAT THE FUK DOES MUNICH HAVE TO DO WITH ANYTHING? You can only hear that kind of talk in some place where people pine over classical American vamps, where judges comb their hair with two-foot combs . . ."

"Mr. Doopeyduk," Hangup said, "surely you're putting our audience on. Why, I never saw a nun raping a hun in Bronxville. Are you sure you're not fantasizing?"

"Man, you can put your psychic elbows and shoulders

in the way and block like a (beep) if you want to—but
I don't think it's funny. I mean, if you keep on talking
about Bronxville and places that don't even exist, the
place will be turned out. Pure and simple. Every damned
cobweb will be ripped to shreds."

"Mr. Doopeyduk," the Hangup said, "we've had some
weird customers up here on the show. Richard Nixon
was on once discussing federal dog-napping legislation
and so was a man who thought he had visited Mars. But
you, Mr. Doopeyduk, by far are the most bizarre."

"I don't have time for tricks. I've spent the whole
week studying watercloset seat covers and I'd just as
soon go back to my work if you don't mind. I think that
I'll hat up anyway because you don't seem to be willing
to run it down front."

I walked out of the studio as a commercial for Radio
Free Europe was quickly put on. Two minutes of barbed
wire and Spike Jones playing "Ave Maria." I was shook
from the interview. I mean, didn't this kat know that he's
living in a freak? If he doesn't, somebody ought to pull
his coat.

The next evening I ran up the stairs, my tuxedo draped
over my arm. Once inside the room, I washed, shaved,
dressed, put fresh Band-Aids on the craggy bruises which
covered my face, applied iodine to swollen areas of my
neck and wrists. I tried to do something for the lopsided
nose and small slit that ran above my right eyelid.

A rap at the door was followed by Elijah's voice. "Hey,
man, there's SOMETHING down here who wants to see
you, looks like a strange-looking beast."

It must be one of HARRY SAM's drivers, I thought.
"Tell him I'll be right down, Elijah."

A man was standing at the bottom of the stairs. At

least I took him to be a man because he wore a derby
and smoked a black cigar; otherwise he was so short, he
could have been a child. He wore a white smock, and
bow tie of polka dots and butterflies.

"You Bukka Doopeyduk?" he asked.

"Yes," I answered him. "You must be one of HARRY
SAM's assistants?"

"That's me," the little man said. "We have to join the
others down at the boat, what's locked up at the pier."

We went out of the house and climbed into an old
Pontiac. I carried the black attaché case crammed full of
notes on my knee. "Do you mind if I open the window?"
I said to the derby, barely showing above the front seat
of the car. I was choking on the smoke issuing from the
cigar, in thick black bunches.

"Go ahead," the little man said, steering the car, its
sirens screaming terror at the stricken passers-by.

"Gee," I said, leaning forward and gripping my knees,
"I can't wait until I get there and engage those bishops
in a discussion of the Nazarene apocalypse."

The man slammed on his brakes, almost sending me
flying over the seat of the car. "Look. If you don't mind,
I would appreciate it if you cut out the yap. I don't go
for all the yakkity-yak while drivin' the customers up to
SAM's. Unnerstand? I mean, I'm not innerstead in your
'pinions so if you want to go shooting off your trap,
then swim the Black Bay to the party," the little man
fumed.

"I get the message," I answered, leaning back into the
cushions of the seat. Peppery little fellow, I thought, as
we drove the rest of the way in silence.

We reached the pier where the plumbers' battleships
had been decorated for the occasion. We climbed out of

the car and jaunted up the ramp to the ship. There was a spattering of applause as some of my fans recognized me.

My escort disappeared into the shadows, leaving me inside the stateroom with some of the guests—which included most of the nothing elements: Nazarene apprentices, Nazarene Bishops, judges and their manicurists, mechanical drawers, and Stephen Wolinski, the mayor of Buffalo, who had left the rest of his party atop the Empire State Building while he accepted an invitation to meet the Chief of State. The guests were doing a dance called the stomp which involved smashing your foot or kinda lifting it and merely stompin'.

In his hand, the mayor held a gift-wrapped kabalsa. Some of the others moved around the edges of the room in their own thing: hands in pockets and doing a mean blasé stomp.

The guests were being entertained by a group of rock-and-roll Nazarene apprentices from the Lower East Side who were playing recorders, lutes, drums, tambourines and electric guitars. They had taken the poems of Ralph Waldo Emerson, Henry Wadsworth Longfellow, Henry David Thoreau—all white men with three names, dead many years—and set them to music.

Songs such as "Look at Dat Waterfowl Bending Its Skinny Neck in da Crick Ovah Dere," "Ain't Nature Grand?" or "Your Cock Was Nevah So Good but When I Laid Ya in the Calabash Field" rang out with authority over the Black Bay.

I leaned over the rail; NOTHING slipping out of sight before me as the boat picked up anchor and began its arduous push toward the island. It felt as if we were moving above the smooth slime of the Black Bay. I could

see the old men trudging homeward after a day of clip-
ping out articles from the old *Harper's Brothers* magazine
led by a spright-stepping octogenarian beating a bass
drum.

In Soulsville the busted microphones resounded with
the oratory of live ghosts protesting the mystery of the
missing children.

Finally, midway through our journey the public-ad-
dress system announced: "Ladies and gentlemen, the
infamous Black Bay." Huge yellow lights from the battleship aimed their beams on the nefarious waters. As far as
the eye could see, long serpentine tentacles oscillated in
the bay and what appeared to be white arms reached
from beneath its surface. The silhouettes of peculiar-
shaped animals leaped into the air—sometimes many feet
high. It was a staggering sight.

People poured from the stateroom, eager to get a better view. Two well-tailored men stood next to me. The
men removed field glasses from cases and looked in fas-
cination upon the waters—writhing with odd life. They
spoke. "I've always had a strange attraction to it, Waldo,"
the first man said. "It's been the subject of a ten-thou-
sand-page report by the International Geophysical Expe-
dition and the Royal Academy of Sciences. Fleets of
oceanographers, a special group called the Black Bay
Authorities, have examined it."

"How did it get thataway, Matthew?" responded the
other man. (Both of whom looked like the grim sabled
brothers on the famous cough-drop box.)

"It's become a veritable Madagascar of the sea, yield-
ing animals not to be found anywhere else in the world.
It seems that in the bad old days the sea was saturated
with chemicals coming from the rows of cereal factories

that lined the banks. There was no cause for alarm until one day a man was peacefully fishing when a bird rose from the waters and carried away his head in its beak. When the British Museum caught the bird—burning its wings with napalm from a supersonic jet—they dissected it and found it to be full of old Manhattan telephone numbers and skulls. An investigation was immediately launched by Congress. You remember the celebrated bird hearings of the fifties. It was decided that it was merely a crowd delusion. The chairman—a dwarf named Eberett Whimplewopper—did such a fine job that he gained a judgeship in HARRY SAM.

"Science had the last say, however. Science took samples from the bay and put them under microscopes. We had decided that crowd delusions were for the more backward unsophisticated part of the world and that we as hardheaded empiricists could never indulge anything that was not amenable to sensory investigation. Since SAM went up there about thirty years ago and took up residence in the er . . . er . . . er . . . way station, the material that flushes into the bay from those huge lips has stirred even stranger forms of life. That sickness he has must be HORRIBLE. Now it's only safe to cross the thing in a battleship."

No sooner had he said that when a giant tentacle attacked the ship, tilting it to an angle. An ever-ready gun, one of four massive ones on the ship, swung into action and blasted the tentacle to bits. Chunks of quivering blob rained down on some of the passengers. The two men plucked some of the trembling membrane-like substance from their clothes where it had fastened itself, and calmly walked back into the stateroom.

Heavy kats, I thought. The battleship docked at a wharf

that stood at the bottom of the great stone wall which surrounded the entire island. The bottom of the wall seemed to disappear into the very depths of the insidious Black Bay. Holding a flashlight, the two men, Waldo and Matthew, led the guests down the ramp.

Suddenly Matthew trained his light on a tentacle lying across the wharf like a lazy boa constrictor with suction holes for scales. Matthew removed a bottle from his pocket and poured its contents on the tentacle. A great groan was heard from the bottom and the passengers held each other to avoid falling from the rocking wharf. The tentacle slunk back into the dreadful waters.

Some steps led from the wharf to the top of the wall where a path began and wound to the summit of the mountain where the motel stood. At the top of the steps a woman waited. She seemed to be dressed in the traditional habit of a nun. I was the last passenger to walk down the ramp and onto the wharf. To the right of me the pounding and crashing of the ugly effervescence of a sickly yellow color could be heard pouring into the bay from the stony mouth of the nineteenth President of the United States.

At the top of the steps the woman greeted us, that is, greeted all of us save Waldo and Matthew, who strode past her with their noses upturned.

"Glad to make your acquaintanceship, I'm sure," she said to the rest of us in authentic Flatbush. "My name is Lenore and I'm the official hostess and cook up here at SAM's. If you'll just walk up this path . . . ," she said, pointing to a cobblestoned path that disappeared around the bend where a gnarled tree stood, its limbs lit up with yellow eyes.

She stood to the side as the guests filed past her on the

path. I was the last to walk by the place where she stood. "Did you say your name was Lenore?" I asked.

"That's right," she said. "The same."

"Do you know an old man named Alfred who spends his time at the Seventeen Nation Disarmament Conference Bar cutting out articles from the old *Harper's Brothers Weekly?*"

"Yes, Alfred is my ex-old man," she said. "You see those creeps walking ahead of everybody else, looking so proper and all? They ruined it."

"Ruined what?" I asked.

"They ruined my romance with Alfred. Prying and sticking their noses into our business. They were all on the rowing team together, Harvard, eighty-nine, and used to carouse about 'wenching,' as they called it, in some of the bars in the dilapidated section of BAWSTON.

"You should have seen Alfred with his features of classical cut, his brow so trim—and his mouth so precise. See I was working behind the BAWR and he'd flirt with me, calling me stuff like the second Helen of Troy and names of dames that guys use to fight those dragons over. Well, Matthew and Waldo, those unalterable bores, had to put their two cents in. Those flat moralistic cough drops. They didn't approve of me and they kicked him off the rowing team and stopped inviting him to the cockfights. When we got hitched the Anglican Church refused to perform the wedding. It was very lonely playing whist every night and when he bumped into his friends on the street—those that would talk to him—spoke in French. Well, Alfred and I became bored with each other after a while but I didn't want to leave him because he was so helpless. Sometimes he would go out into the streets with nothing but a boiled

vest and tall hat and carrying a pocket watch that
stopped on August 6, 1945. I didn't mind the perms he
used to read me but I was young and wanted to do a
little boo-ga-loo so I asked him to buy me some harpsichord lessons. On the pretense of taking the harpsichord
lessons, I went down into the Village and met the black
man named Jr. Bug and we did the boo-ga-loo for days.
Finally Waldo and Matthew who were in a café on
Greenwich Avenue doing strange recipes spotted me even
though I was wearing shades.

"They told Alfred and he took me to court. We appeared before Judge Whimplewopper, a little fellow so
high who combs his hair in public with a two-foot-long
comb."

"Yes, I've had dealings with him," I said, interrupting
her.

"Well, anyway, the Civil Liberties Committee warned
him that the decision would make American justice a
laughingstock around the world but he went ahead and
did it."

"Did what?" I asked impatiently.

"He admitted all the precedents from the Salem witch
trials where these teeny boppers were burned at the stake
for going out into the woods to meet black men. I was
due to be burned at the stake too.

"The villagers were led by J. Lapp Swine, jazz critic
from the *Deformed Demokrat*, who romped about rousing the mob with a small torchlight between his toes.
Being a double-jointed freak, he was capable of all kinds
of odd contortions.

"Suddenly a man in a black limousine, with the symbol of the Great Commode on its license plates, pulled
up. It was Judge Whimplewopper. He intervened and

said, 'Instead of burning this tomato at the stake, we're going to send her up to SAM's place in exile, where she will be condemned to deliver up cruel and strange recipes for the Chief.'"

"What recipes?" I asked.

"That's classified," she replied. "The funny thing is," she said as we rounded the last bend before the top of the mountain, "one night I found those Catholic rejects Matthew and Waldo up here doing the same thing I'm doing, with all their might."

"Cooking strange recipes?" I asked.

"You might put it that way," she smiled.

What stood before us at the summit of the mountain was one magnificent sight. The Harry Sam Motel rose so high that it pushed the clouds aside. The helicopters whirred above, dipping in and out. They were marked with the symbol of the Great Commode. It was a giant Victorian house with gables and bay windows. It stood there harsh and forbidding in the moonlight.

Inside the ballroom the guests continued their stomp. On the walls were giant black hoopla hoops. Some women had engaged me in a conversation about BE-COMINGS. Standing there with a cocktail in my hand, I had just gotten to the part "trees lifting their leafy arms to pray" when someone tapped me on the shoulder.

PART V

The Last One on the Block to Know

It was the tiny man in the white smock. "Are you Bukka Doopeyduk?" he asked in a strident voice.

"The same," I said, glancing at the women who were giving me streaks of white teeth.

"Follow me," the little man said, "the boss wants to see you." The women began to gabble anxiously as the man glided from the room as if on wheels.

"Just a minute, sir. I have to pick up my attaché case chock full of notes."

The man twirled about and flicking some ashes from the big cigar said, "Okay, but quit stallin'. I ain't got all day. Whaddaya think this is, Fredrichsbach or some joint?"

We were joined in the hall by two Screws in those long black capes. They escorted me into a splendid library where the two Screws sat on a sofa and the little

man beckoned me to sit at a great garish maple table
in the center of the room.

"Would you like some likker?"

"Don't mind if I have a little taste of brandy," I said,
relaxing in a black leather club chair with my fingers
inside my suspenders.

He went to a bookshelf as I lit up a Picayune cigarette.
On the other side of the bookshelf was a bar. After removing some implements from the shelves he began to
shake a mixer vigorously. I suddenly felt dizzy.

"Hey, what's going on here?" I asked.

"Relax," the tiny man said, stirring the drink. "We're
taking you for a little ride."

THE LIBRARY WAS MOVING! I could not determine
from sensation whether it was moving up or down. It
seemed to be speeding through the universe like some
demon missile. I took a taste of brandy and before long
dozed off. It seemed like centuries before the elevator
came to a halt. The Screws and the little man put on gas
masks. Then the little man—after providing me with one
—walked to bookshelves which covered an entire wall.
He pressed a button and the shelves began to move from
left to right. I could not believe what I beheld when the
shelves finally disappeared into the side wall.

Before me, in a high black wheelchair flanked on each
side by seven little men dressed like my escort, sat a man
with a blanket over his knees. Behind him stood the
Chief of Screws, the Chief of the Nazarene Bishops,
Nancy Spellman, the Chief Theoretician of the Party
and the Chairman of the Joint Chiefs of Staff (known
by the ancients as SNATANACHIA, AGALIAREPT,
FLEUTEREETY, AND SAGATANAS). Behind them
was a high toilet booth with a diamond-studded knob

on its door of carved griffins and gargoyles. It was surrounded on each side by seven smaller black and more austere little booths. Everybody wore gas masks and stood at attention except for the man in the wheelchair who held the neck of a bottle in the opening of his gas mask.

"Bukka Doopeyduk," the little man said, putting the *Buck* magazine under his arm. "MEET SAM."

"PUT ER DERE BUKKA GLAD TO MEET YOUSE."

I dropped to my knees between the two elite Screws standing at attention. It can't be, I thought. The great dictator, former Polish used-car salesman and barn burner.

"Gimme some skin dere, kid." The little man returned to an empty place in line.

"Thanks for bringing the lad, you little Rapunzel, you," twitted Nancy, Chief Nazarene Bishop.

The little man turned around suddenly and whipped out a .45, aiming it right into the Bishop's face. "Another crack like that and I'll lob you right back into MARBLE COLLEGIATE CHURCH."

"CUT IT OUT, YOU GUYS," said the opening in the gas mask. "Can't you see I'm trying to speak to this sturdy young lad about what's going down in ME. So quiet before I blast both of youse."

"All right, boss, but next time I'm going to give it to him."

"Shake hands, my boy," SAM said in a raspy froggy-the-gremlin voice.

I extended my trembling hand to his and then pulled it away, leaving a stringy wad of goo between our fingers. He wiped his hand on his shirt.

"Excuse me, my boy, you see I have this weird ravaging illness which causes it to melt on my hands and in my

mouth too. Causes it to melt in my mouth and on my
hands too," he laughed spastically, turning to the men
standing behind him, giving the Chairman of the Joint
Chiefs of Staff a poke in the ribs.

"Gee, boss, that's real funny," the men in the room
said in chorus.

I finally managed to speak. "HARRY SAM, my leader,
O what I gonna do? I'm so very overwhelmed."

"Call me SAM, kid, dish the formalities. You're just as
good as me or even better. Just for being such a gent,
I'm going to give you one of my ball-point pens," he
said, removing one of twelve from his shirt pocket and
giving it to me.

"Gee, I don't know what to say, SAM," I said, looking
at the boots which rested on the wheelchair's footboards
below the blanket. One boot appeared to be larger than
the other.

"He's got real class, ain't he, boys?"

"Like somethin' out of the Knickerbocker Follies,"
SAM's mouthpieces chimed.

"You know, Bukka," he said, "just because I've been up
here evacuating for thirty years from the really way-out
bring-down illness doesn't mean that I don't know what's
going on down in ME. Why, I look through my binoculars and see everything flying over there in NOTHING
which is ME. NOTHING escapes my eyes. I like the
way you operate. Here, have one of the pauses what re-
freshes, har, har, har, har," he said, jamming the bottle's
neck into my mouth.

He belched, wiped his mouth with the back of his
hand, then continued. "Now there's a lot of clammering
and beefing going on down there. Some of those dropouts
are griping about me not coming out of the John to hold

them in my lap. A man in my position can't be exposing himself in public. I'm not nice to be near."

The Chairman of the Joint Chiefs of Staff winked at the Chief Nazarene Bishop through his goggles, nodding in agreement, pinched his nozzle and pointed to the back of SAM's bald head. "YOU GUYS TRYING TO BE FUNNY OR SOME-THING? I TOLE YOU NOTHIN' ESCAPES MY EYES. YOU REMEMBER WHAT HAPPENED TO THOSE JOKERS WHAT WAS TRYING TO JAM UP THE PLUMBING WITH DEM CHICKEN FEATHERS? YOU WANT SOME OF THE SAME MEDICINE?" he said, bringing out a German luger from beneath the blanket.

"We was only greeing with youse, boss," said the Joint Chiefs of Staff Chairman, his face livid with fear.

"WHEN I WANT YOU TO AGREES OR DIS-AGREES WIT ME, I'M DA ONE GIVES DA ORDERS, UNNERSTAND?"

"We gotcha boss," the four replied, mopping their brows with their hands and wringing the sweat to the tile floor.

"You gotta watch these eggheads," he said, again turning to me. "The only thing they're good for is handin' out honorary degrees to my generals and Screws, on commencement day at all the Harry Sam Universities. You should see these shirkers. Why, one of dem guys is pushing a ball of shit all over the world by the tip of his nose."

"The paper is called 'The Egyptian Dung Beetle in Kafka's "Metamorphosis," ' " added the little man whose head was now buried in the daily racing form.

"Yeah, somethin' like that," answered SAM. "See, they

push them little mega-morphosis all over the world for me and I give um peanuts and then they start signing petitions and debatin' them white papers what me and the boys hustle up once in a while to keep peace and harmony down there and cut out all the yakkity-yak. That's why I had to send them gray ladies down there that time."

"One time we developed a thing what would put down all them smart-aleck spicks acting up called . . . 'The Counter Insurgency Foundation,'" said the little man, biting into an apple.

"Yeah, and this foundation came up wit some weapon what would crush them spicks and had them yellow dwarfs with pocketknives running around giggling and hopping around, har, har, har, har. You shoulda seen them running with their clothes all on fire, har, har, har, har," said HARRY SAM, slapping his knees. "What was that weapon called, Rapunzel?" asked SAM of the little man.

"I think we called it a beneficent incapacitor."

"Well, them guys was applying for that foundation in droves, then they got the noive to get up there in their hats and gowns singing 'Blow—he ain't much eager to' at the top of their lungs."

"Gaudeamus igitur," corrected the little man.

"There's one of them guys what a famous 'tomic scientist. Little fellow with ice-cold blue eyes over at Princeton Institute of Advanced Studies. You shoulda seen him at Yukka Flats that morning with his clammy hands all over my detonator. Why, he wouldn't even let my generals get *their* cookies he was carrying on so, quotin' perms and stuff. See, they laugh at me because on the newsreels, my shorts don't fit too good."

"We think they fit fine, boss. You look like Rock Hudson," the chorus said.

"No, you're wrong, boys," SAM said. "Gravity has gotten the best of me and I'm a little flabby and sick and not pleasant to be near, but them guys go around posing all day, talking about ethical . . . ethical . . ."

"Ethical neutrality," my little escort said. But before he could continue the Chief Nazarene Bishop started for the little man's throat and soon they were rolling about the tile floor, fighting. The other little men and the remaining chiefs encircled them, rooting for their favorite.

Finally SAM said, "STOP IT! STOP IT! WHAT'S COME OVER YOU GUYS? GET UP OFF DAT FLOOR!" The men rushed back to their places in line, except for the little man who was slowly brushing off his smock and staring at the Chief Bishop evilly.

"Next time you do that, I'm going to drown you in the Black Bay—preacher or no preacher," the annoyed little man threatened.

"Shaddup both of youse. One more crack and I'll plug you," SAM said. "Now, what's the matter wit youse, preacher?"

"Well, sniff, sniff," answered the Bishop Nancy Spellman, "you said I could be the one allatime comment on ethics but each time I try to say somethin', he's always puttin' his two cents in."

"Look, preacher, do you want to go back to Marble Collegiate and sell mustard seeds to a bunch of sexless Sunoco Oil widows?"

"No, SAM. I'm very happy up here giving up strange and exotic recipes," the Bishop replied.

"That's more like it," said Sam. "Now where was I?" he said, turning once again to me.

"You were talking about ethical neutrality," I answered.

"My philosophy," SAM said, smashing his fist into his open palm, "is when they act up or give you some lip, bomb the fuken daylights out of um. When my ol man's roosters give him some cackle, that would fix um every time. That's the only thing they understand. And that goes for spicks and gooks and all the rest what ain't like us. Why, it would be no skin off my nose if all the Chinamen in the world got stuck in a dumbwaiter. Saving face and fulfilling your commitments, making alliances with da Arabs and all dem other baggy pants you can trust is okay. But if you don't stop the others where they are, before ya know it, they'll be surrounding NOTHIN' which is ME like a bunch of Free-Lance Pallbearers.

"Step up here and feel that muscle, Bukka." He rolled up his sleeve and revealed a lump nudging the crease at his elbow. I was a bit nervous but SAM assured me. I put my hand on the lump. It was as hard as a rock. "Gee SAM, that's sure powerful," I said.

"Every night when we go to bed, we is thankful for that lump, boss," the chorus said.

"That is what you call 'intestinal fortitude' as we use to say down in the Republican Club in the perfumed stockade. But it won't last. You see, I'm getting old, Bukka. Maybe forty years from now you can have the job. The top-secret specialty what keeps me alive is bound to run out but as long as I'm dictator of ME . . ." his voice rising and pounding his thumb into his chest so hard that the gas mask shuddered, "elected in free and democratic elections, I'll do my best to improve NOTHING.

"Now I been looking out these glasses at Soulsville and

I'm not happy with what I see. The people seem to have a lot of FRUSTRATION, ANXIETY and DESPAIR down there. I know all about that; I read *the ny whine* every day. But this stuff is taken a nasty turn. Last week some hoodlums attacked my friend Eclair Porkchop and I had to bring him up here until the heat was off. They nearly kilt the preacher. He's been on the phone upstairs trying to get Miles Davis to translate the Bible. But I don't think that's going to save his neck. Back in the old days he use to go out in the snow rounding up votes for old SAM. He use to spellbound them colored people saying 'Glory' and stuff—even taught me to say it—GLORY, GLORY, GLORY, GLORY, GLORY, JEEEEEEEEEE-EESSSSSSSSUUUUUUUSSSSSSSSSUSSSSS. I SEE DAT OLE WHEEL TURNING IN THE SKY," SAM said, waving his arms.

"LET THE CHURCH SAY AMEN AND HELP ME LAWDY," said the chorus.

"But now I think he's lost his drive, that certain spark. Seems a little gumless and stick-to-itiveness without. I want you to take that job. Go down there in Soulsville and tell them IT'S GOIN' BE ALL RIGHT, BY AND BY IN THE SKY."

"Say it again, SAM," I said, not wanting to jumble my first assignment as Nazarene Bishop. I was overjoyed!

"Now we want you to have breakfast with us tomorrow and we can discuss the details. After which Lenore the maid will show you the grounds. Show him to a room," SAM said to one of the Screws standing next to me.

I rose and said, "Thank you, HARRY SAM, former Polish used-car salesman and barn burner."

"Don't mention it, Bukka. I like your spunk. You re-

mind me of myself. Why, I sit here all day readin'
Ernest Hemingway and practicing strange out-of-the-way
dishes."

"Thanks again, SAM," I said, following the Screws
into the mobile library.

"Don't take no wooden nickels and if you do, name
him after me, har, har, har, har, har, har, har . . ."
was the last thing HARRY SAM said as the bookshelf
moved from the side of the wall.

"Honest to Pete, boss. You're a regular summer festival," said the chorus.

The ascent, unlike the trip down, took about five minutes. The Screws led me out of the library into the hall
near the ballroom. The thunder streaked into the trees
which, gnarled and macabre, stood outside the garden
doors. The shutters slammed violently throughout the
house. The hoopla hoops bounced against the wall. Eerie
organ music came somewhere from the very roof of the
house. There was no sign of the gay crowd. Having
stomped up a storm the party guests had flit.

Upstairs in the huge guest room I decided to spend
the night going over lines to be delivered to the audience
of Soulsville. "IT'S GOING TO BE ALL RIGHT, BY
AND BY IN THE SKY. . . . IT'S GOING TO BE ALL
RIGHT, BY AND BY IN THE SKY."

But I couldn't concentrate; my mind was still aglow
from the wonderful news from the summer's festival. I
lay in the bed with my hands supporting my head,
dreaming about what direction my career would take.
What would the other Nazarene apprentices think of
me now? A Bishop of Soulsville and only twenty-three. I
would be one of the youngest, if not the youngest, Bishop

in the history of out-of-sight. I rose and went to a mirror. Primping and preening myself I reflected on what kind of Bishop I would be.

Would I be stern and aloof but benevolent to my constituency? Or would I be the gregarious type, indiscriminately mingling with all sections of the population, dipping my fork into their pots of collard greens and hog maws—to show how, after all, I too was of humble origins and had "soul"?

SAM had no real hard-and-fast rule about celibacy. In fact most of the Nazarene Bishops were celibate by inclination rather than by dogma or coercion. Think of the international beauties on my arm as I strolled through Soulsville telling everyone, "IT'S GOING TO BE ALL RIGHT, BY AND BY IN THE SKY. . . . IT'S GOING TO BE ALL RIGHT, BY AND BY IN THE SKY!"

I was lost in thought as the shadows gave way to complete darkness and the wind rustled through the yellow-eyed trees. The moonlight bathed the room.

At first it was a short irregular noise somewhat like a whimper; a muffled quick moan. Then it became louder, adding wails and high-pitched screams—like the night sounds of the tropics. Someone was in trouble, I thought, removing a turkey musket from a rack on the wall of the guest room.

Tying the rope of my robe around me, I rushed into the hall. The noise seemed to be emanating from below the first floor of the building. I ran down the stairs past the ballroom and parted the curtains in front of the library. But instead of a door there was a solid mass of steel. At the other end of the hall there were four other doors, all marked "classified."

I opened the one nearest to me, and out walked Waldo

and Matthew, who continued arm in arm gently up the
stairs, Waldo saying to Matthew, "Not since the Tu Fu
dynasty has there been such an outpouring of creativity,
such a potpourri of form; and those monsoons are worth
more than twenty volumes of haiku, and all of Snyder
and Williamsville, New York, are full of the pixie-quick
tracks of their sandals. There is no hope for the Pope.
O, what is to become of us?"

"Hey, can't you hear that person screaming downstairs? THIS IS NO TIME TO BE TALKING ABOUT
PERMS."

But the men had disappeared at the top of the steps.
I pulled at the door of the next room as grunts, groans
and squeals continued to come from below. The door
slowly opened, its rusty hinges squeaking. Before me
were concrete steps that disappeared into the hollow of
an abysmal throat. The moans were definitely coming
from that oval-shaped darkness.

Putting my finger on the trigger of the turkey musket
I started down the endless steps. Through the soles of
my shoes I could feel the concrete; the slime of tiny
animals squashed underfoot and rats dashed across my
shoestrings. Wispy spider webs brushed against my face
as I pushed on—my ankles moving through sludge—
until I came nearer to the gasps and snorts echoing
through the dank ol house steeped in mildew. When
I came to the middle landing an awful stench attacked
my brain that smelled of the very putrescence of mass
graves. I took a handkerchief and held it to my nose as
I ran through the passageways and past propped-up
human skeletons in chains. I finally came to a door,
behind which, shouts and wails nearly burst my ear-
drums. I broke it open and saw on the tiled floor men

in grotesque pretzel-shaped poses. It was a kind of underground cockfight. One man jumped up and covering his face ran and hid under the sink.

"MAN, AM I THE ORIGINAL FALL GUY? I GOT A GOOD MIND TO BLAST YOU MOTHAFUKAS RAT SMACK INTO THOSE CRYSTALS WHIRLING ABOVE OUR HEADS."

HARRY SAM jumped to his feet and hobbled toward me. Wiping his lips with the back of his hand and zipping up his fly, he shouted, "WHAT-IS-DA MEANIN' OF INTERRUPTIN' MY GOAT-SHE-ATE-SHUNS?"

"Get over there against the wall, SAM," I said, banging the barrel of the gun against his stomach.

"NOW SEE HERE, WISE GUY, I'M DA BOSS UP HERE. I GIVE DA ORDERS."

I lifted the musket and aimed for the area between his eyes.

"BUT I'M ALWAYS WILLING TO COMPROMISE SO I'LL GET MY TAIL OVER THERE AGAINST THAT WALL. JUST THIS ONCE."

"What do you have to say for yourself?" I said to the first nude man who sat on the cold tile.

bong bong bong bong

"Well, Bukka, it kinda go like this—C E G D. I was up here 'gotiatin' one night when the sweet old man put his hot hand on my knee. Before I knew it, it had gotten good to me and I was on my hands and knees doing the salty dog with all my might."

"Okay, Eclair Porkchop," I said to the first man. "I can forgive passion. What are you doing up here turning tricks? You're supposed to be a CREATOR," I said to the second man.

"It's like this, Bukka," the man answered. "These tricks

pay more than my hoopla hoops so I come up here once in a while and give up some head. No big thing. I never said those hoopla hoops were art. It was SAM who made it art. He and his washroom attendants control the museums so as long as they were forking over the bread I made them hoopla hoops. The only reason I got into the business was that one day the hoopla hoops were sliding down over my thighs and SAM was digging through the telescope gettin' his jollies. That night a limousine came to my loft and brought me up here where SAM introduced me to some of the most powerful people in art circles. Finally I had such a demand for hoopla hoops that they began selling them in the A&P."

I sensed something creeping up behind me. I swung around bashing SAM on the head so hard that he dropped the toilet chain he held in his hand and fell against the wall. He slumped unconscious to the tile, his tongue sticking out and his eyes crossed. Turning from Cipher I walked over to the sink where another man was cowering beneath its base near the plumbing. I forced his hand from his face. It couldn't be—NOSETROUBLE?

"O, BUKKA, MERCY, SPARE ME. I ALWAYS WANTED TO DO IT, SEE HOW IT FELT AND WHEN THEY SENT ME UP HERE TO NEGOTIATE FOR THE MISSING TOTS I JUMPED AT THE CHANCE. O, BUKKA, I TOSSED AND TURNED IN MY BED FOR YEARS AND YEARS AND FINALLY THE DAY ARRIVED AND I CAME UP TO MEET THIS DIRTY OLD MAN IN PERSON AND HE JUST SENT THRILLS ALL UP AND DOWN MY SPINE AND MADE ME SCREAM WITH ALL MY BEING."

I started to blow the mothafuka to kingdom come but

suddenly the house shook at its very roots. I turned and saw that HARRY SAM, having recovered, was pulling a cord that hung near the door. He then screamed in rhythmic incantation: "Enter—Wand and Wayside; Up—Warrior Watchman and Wing; Up—Witness; Run—Digest Dazzle Deacon and Debut; Rush—Drummer Dresser and Dasher."

The doors of the little johns swung open and the gnomes began to rise from their seats. I started for the exit, backpedaling with my turkey musket until I came to the door where SAM was crouched on the floor. "IT'S CURTAINS FOR YOU, BUSTER. YOU'LL NEVER GET AWAY FROM HERE! LISTEN AT DEM TROOPS COMIN' DOWN DA STAIRS AND LOOK AT DEM GNOMES GETTING UP OFF THEIR RUMPS." I hit him in the mouth and blood gushed out.

I opened the door and shut it behind me. "If anyone follows me, I'll blast them to bits," I shouted.

I ran up the steps to the middle ranges and hid in the shadows hoping that the stampede of footsteps now descending upon the bottoms would pass right by me. IT WORKED. Five hundred marines, five hundred navy personnel, five hundred coast guard and five hundred Green Berets plus one Arab, one Nationalist Chinese, one Rhodesian, one Peruvian and one Aussie sped by the middle range. It was a regular U.N. peace-keeping force.

I headed up the steps until I came to the main floor. I ran to the third door marked "classified" and opened it, thinking of the door as a possible exit. Hundreds of tiny skulls poured out and knocked me off my feet. Skulls rolled through the halls and stacked against the walls to pile up slowly. A tide of gore was rising all around

me. I heard the sound of tingly music coming from outside the house. I plodded through the skulls—still bounc-
ing and rushing from the third room—and toward a window where the merry-go-round, connected to the cab of
a big Mack truck, was winding around the path. Behind
the merry-go-round were the rolling waters of the bay
licking the top of the wall like black tongues. In the distance I could see another battleship head back toward
HARRY SAM.

HUNDREDS OF FOOTSTEPS WERE COMING
FROM THE BOTTOMS. IT ALL BECAME CLEAR TO
ME! THE LAST ONE ON THE BLOCK TO KNOW.
I puked and fainted into the heap of bones, dead weight.

When I awoke I found myself being carried down
the path. I looked up into the face of my rescuer, Eclair
Porkchop.

"Man, you weigh as much as lead," said the preacher,
running down the path toward the high wall. We had
passed the gnarled tree standing in the middle of the
road when voices of the mob could be heard pouring
out of the motel. The helicopters dipped and started
toward us.

"What are you doing rescuing me? You're with them."

"No time to talk now. You have to get away from
here," he replied.

We finally reached the Black Bay which had hungrily
rose above Rutherford Birchard Hayes's head and now
was on level with the top of the wall.

Suddenly two Screws came from out of the darkness.

"JUMP, BOY, JUMP!" the preacher said.

"But the Latin roots, those terrible man-eating plants
and who knows what else," I pleaded.

He whispered into my ear and gave me a small bottle, just as two Screws grabbed him by the arms, then aimed two lugers at me. Pouring the bottle's contents into the water before me, I dove into the Black Bay, which now showed crystal-clear, with brilliant-colored vegetation and fancy fish swimming at the bottom. Some distance out I turned over and began a backstroke. I could see the motel at the top of the mountain, its "EATS" sign blinking rapidly.

On the oak tree which stood on the last bend of the pathway near the wall, a flaming figure swung back and forth. A mob had gathered below. They were playing dogbones and kazoos and blowing into jugs the popular American song "There'll Be a Hot Time in the Old Town Tonight." I wept; tears pouring down my cheeks and into the water, but having business to take care of I could not pause—I turned around and kept on swimming.

I clutched the branch of a tree which drooped into the Black Bay. The ol men in the Emperor Franz Joseph Park scooped up arms full of film and slammed shut the bound copies of *Harper's Brothers Weekly*. They sent clouds of dust and the musty smell of pulp up from the park.

They said, "Whoopie, yeserie," and jogging erlong, swapped "do-si-dos" and "I told you so's" and they zigzagged, reeled and rocked in file all around the park until meeting two-by-two and side-by-side they marched into the tree-lined street of ol brownstones where an ol man was dropped at every stoop until there was only the bony-kneed soul with the bass drum—he boomed with a ragged soupbone—and then soon he too was gone as wheelbarrows of dentures, toupees, elevator shoes and sloppily laid corpses stood before each ol man's home.

[Da efficient widow executioners had raised dem black-
checkered flags right on time, baby. *And dat was all she
wrote cause da pencil broke* for those fuked-up souls—rest
in peace for 1931–1939.]

I saw an object atop the fragments of dead clippings.
I waded up to my knees through the grassy film and
the phlegm-covered flags and picked up an ivory music
box. On the cover done in mother-of-pearl was a picture
of Lenore in her Bickford's uniform. I opened the music
box and heard the tape of the familiar voice:

> ROGER YOUNG IN THE FIRST AT SARATOGA
> ROGER YOUNG IN THE NINTH AT CHURCHILL DOWNS
> ROGER YOUNG IN THE FOURTH AT BATAVIA
> ROGER YOUNG IN THE FIFTH AT AQUEDUCT
> ANNOUNCED BY RAPUNZEL

Why those sneaky old bastards in the Seventeen Nation Disarmament gin mill, I chuckled, putting us on
for all these years—pretending to be Nazarene patriots,
but actually bettin' on the nags!

My shirt was wringing wet and barracudas wiggled
from under my pants cuffs. I looked at my pocket watch.
It had stopped at 3:00 A.M., August 6, 1945—when the
skulls pressing against my thighs had crushed its glass
plate.

THROUGH THE PARK TOWARD SOULSVILLE I
RAN, MY FEET SLAPPING (PING-PING) THE PAVE-
MENT AS I RAN TOWARD THE "FOUR CORNERS".
INTERSECTION IN THE MIDDLE OF SAM WHERE
VIOLENT WHIRLPOOLS OF PEOPLE SEEMED TO
BE HEADING PELL-MELL INTO THE CROSS-
ROADS. I RAN ACROSS THE STREET JUST AS A

T-MODEL FORD COMING FROM AN OPPOSITE
DIRECTION SWERVED TO AVOID HITTING ME.
I HAD NOT CHANCED TO LOOK BACK UPON
THE RESULTING EXPLOSION WHICH SENT
SCREWS AND A PRIZE DOG, AN OL WOMAN, A
FORMER MOVIE STAR, A SLUM LORD AND AS-
SISTANT, HANDICAPPED VETERANS, AKESTRA OF
MEN IN WHITE FORMALS AND A TOP GOVERN-
MENT OFFICIAL AND WIFE FLOATING UP FROM
THE STREET HALOED AND WHITE-ROBED AND
STRUMMING HARPS.

When I reached the projects the lights of the auditorium located in the community center was ablaze. Outside the center a sign announced the reason:

COMMUNITY MEETING
WHERE ARE OUR CHILDREN?
speakers discussions committees
symposiums Kool-Aid & lemonade

I stood in the back of the auditorium. M/Neighbor
was speaking to the audience from a lectern which stood
on the stage.

"Folks, Nosetrouble be back directly from his gotiating
with SAM—but in the meantime how about a few frank
pranks?" He began to slap his thighs and fuss with his
trousers as he performed a mean hambone.

"Aw man, quit shuking," said one man, raising himself from a cot in the middle of the auditorium. "We've
been waiting here for two weeks now and the kat hasn't
come back and all you do is throw a whole lot of
empty lemonade at people. Now if he doesn't come back
soon we're going to take things into our own hands."

"Have patience, my friends," M/Neighbor said. "I tell

you what I'm going to do. How would you like to meet
a real live ghost? A man who spooked Rutherford Birchard Hayes's biography and is gung ho about the lawd."

"Awwwwwwww ain't that commendable," said some
of the ol sisters. The water pitcher rattled as the first
poltergeist to integrate Cornpone University walked toward the lectern. But having no time for a matinee I
ran down the aisle and jumped to the platform, wresting
the microphone from his hand.

Never one good at diplomacy, I blurted, "LADIES AND
GENTLEMEN, SAM'S EATING YOUR CHILDREN."
The audience gasped. "I mean, I mean . . ." (think-
ing of how brutal the language was), "LADIES AND
GENTLEMEN, SAM HAS A RARE DELICACY YOU
OUGHT TO KNOW ABOUT."

"Man, what are you talking about? Babbling like that,"
M/Neighbor said. "You're supposed to be dead. Look
at what this says," he said, removing a *ny tooth* from
his pocket.

ACTOR MEETS QUEER DEATH IN BLACK BAY
NOSETROUBLE STILL NEGOTIATIN' MISSING CHILDREN
WORLD-WIDE YAM RIOTS BREAK LOOSE
MARINES SENT TO LATIN AMERICA, ASIA AND MOST OF AFRICA
POPE ABDICATES

"Lies," I said. "Nosetrouble is not negotiating anything!
And I'm alive and kicking," I said as a fish jumped from
my pocket and flipped about the stage until it died.

"Now I suppose you're going to tell us you swam the
Black Bay?" M/Neighbor taunted.

"Not only that," I said, "NOSETROUBLE IS UP IN
THE JOHN DOING THIS." I screamed, raising my fist
to my lips and making squishing sounds.

"Aw man, you're just trying to get publicity for your show," M/Neighbor said. "Prove it."

"I'LL PROVE IT!" I said, yanking the sheet from the ghost who blushed and put his hands over his privates. His pubic hairs were shaped into a Smith Brothers' beard giving him away to the audience who began chasing him and M/Neighbor off the stage.

"COME OUTSIDE," I shouted to the audience.

We reached the outside of the auditorium just as the merry-go-round was kinda slipping and easing away from the curb.

"STOP THE MERRY-GO-ROUND! STOP IT!" I shouted.

The women ran and plopped themselves into its path. I leaped to the platform and unscrewed the head of an evil smirking steel droll and placed the infant on the sheet. In another compartment, I found a tape recorder.

ALL HELL BROKE LOOSE!!!

The man helped me as I tried to open the door of the truck's cab. The door was locked. Someone came from the rear of the crowd with a blowtorch. We melted the door open and climbed inside to find an abandoned steering wheel.

Surely the thing didn't drive itself, I thought. I sat on the leather seats as the statue of HARRY SAM in the project park fell with a thunderous THWACK.

Above my head I heard a light scratching sound. I turned around. Behind me were two doors belonging to a cabinet used to store tools and other gear for the merry-go-round. On the front of the door was a pinup picture of Betty Grable. I opened the door while two men stood on each side of the truck. Inside the cabinet, crouching, looking like the cat who had swallowed the canary—grinning and waving at us—was none other than Elijah Raven.

"What are you doing up there, Elijah?" I asked.

"Trickin', Charlie," was the terse reply. "You see, I drive this truck for SAM. Doing a little moonlightin'. Little does he know that I'm collecting box tops from his cereal right under his nose so that when the revolution comes we can pull a Quaker Oats gambit on the kats. Popping from guns, so to speak. Get it, hee, hee, popping from guns."

The two men on the side of the truck were not amused. "You gone have to do better than that, my man," said one.

I left Elijah in the cab of the truck biting his nails and surrounded by the men who were rolling up their sleeves—as Elijah tried to come up with something better than that.

"UP TO SAM'S," I shouted to the crowd, who now believed my discovery of sheer evil. We ran through the vapidness of SAM and to the Emperor Franz Joseph Park, climbing through the ol men's possessions—the colostomy bags, snuff boxes, fake frills and moles. "FOLLOW ME!" I yelled to the crowd that lined the bank. "INTO THE DRINK."

"But those Latin roots," someone said, "those terrible bloodletting plants."

I whispered into the ear of the man standing next to me and told him about the bottle's secret. Pouring the remainder of the bottle into the bay I dove in and started plowing toward the island. Hundreds of splashes registered behind me.

After the seven-mile swim we arrived at the wharf

on the island. People were assisted from the water until everyone stood along the platform.

"Now we'll have to be very quiet," I advised. "The place is heavily guarded."

We walked up the steps and reached the top of the wall. I expected stiff resistance, but to my surprise the pathway leading to the motel was deserted. We moved through the bush until we reached the top of the mountain. A handful of Swiss guards poured out to challenge us. They had been driven from Italy at the height of the Bingo crisis and were given freedom-fighter status in HARRY SAM. After their unemployment checks ran out they were hired as the household guard, the Chief Nazarene Bishop, the theoretician of the party, and the Chief of Screws, having been sent all over the world to put down the Yam insurgencies.

We tore the Swiss guards to pieces, whipping out some of those trapezoidic switchblades (blades dat upon opening spring every which way), and put them on the kats.

No one remained to guard the place but the washroom attendants in the bottoms. We reached the door of the grand John and slowly opened it. HARRY SAM sat in a wheelchair with his back turned to us. He was watching television.

On the screen: the vicar of the Screws, Mr. Nancy Spellman (called on the sly "tail-gunner Nancy" by some Screw pilots) was having his swanky ermine robe and golden girdle rudely removed by some mean-looking Puerto Rican nationalists. Their children were eating Chuchifritos and rolling Nancy's little fat butterball of a severed head around the room. In some unidentified port thousands of plumbers were drowning in oil fires

148 The Free-Lance Pallbearers

while their battleships capsized in the background. In a Peruvian market place natives shoved yams and copper wire down the throat of the Chairman of the Joint Chiefs of Staff until his jaws split open (incendiary yams).

Someplace else five hundred big black Gurkhas were gang banging Lenore who rolled her thighs, popped her fingers and enjoyed every minute of it. She smacked her lips and squirmed like an eel, punctuating these ecstatic cries with the comment, "WOW-EE. This sure doesn't taste like tomato juice."

Da Chief of da Screws was giving his farewell lecture on a scaffold in Leopoldville. He was trying to explain that if they'd release him, he'd have his men learn Puerto Rican and Yoruba—but before he could start loll-gaggin' and handing out white papers the trap door opened, two seconds before his scheduled death, and the kat kinda dropped and with a crraaacccckkkk, his neck snapped.

On another channel Mlle. Matzabald had been caught trying to make it down the Amazon River with a rowboat full of profits reaped from her Anti-Freeze Creplach Shows. The *real* headhunters caught up with her and waving a copy of the *Wall Street Journal* shouted, "Come back here wit dat anti-freeze. Dat ain't yo anti-freeze. Dat's our anti-freeze. We sick and tired of you 'mericans comin' down here carrying off our anti-freeze." They then gave her their version of the now famous Nuremberg War Trials which they called an "Anaconda Flop" (they were still savages, you see)—which simply means that the kat was allowed to row through the Amazon and flop about with them anacondas and after flopping if she still felt like bopping she could join their fires and listen to all the Prestige and Bluenote albums that the headhunters had snatched from all of the deadhead missionaries from NOW-HERE. They wanted to see if she was really that hip.

So you see, things were very very shaky everywhere the eye could scan.

SAM's assistants were running around with hot-water bottles, ice packs and thermometers as they aided the ailing leader. I crept up behind him and put my hands in front of his eyes. He in turn put his fat hand on my wrist. "Is that you Miss Matzabald, come to take my mind off this crisis by giving me some of them good mechanical drawers?"

He started, jerked forward, and sprung to his feet. "Hey! whad's da big idear? You . . ." He continued to pant. "How did you get out of that Black Bay?"

But before I could explain, the gnomes having got wind of their leader's difficulty, rushed out and attacked the crowds. But they were no match for my greasy stompers who mashed them as if they were so many pesky little bugs. Rapunzel was in the corner holding off some wild-eyed bruisers.

"Spare that man," I yelled. "We owe him a lot."

"Look, buster," Rapunzel said. "You don't owe me no favors."

"Come down off your perch, Rapunzel," I insisted. "I know what you did for us and we're eternally grateful."

"I don't know what you're talking about," he said, giving one man a quick-as-a-flash karate chop.

But another man moved in quickly and subdued the gnome. The little creature fought back furiously, even digging his nails into the man's back.

"Hey, wait a minute! Where is SAM?"
While we were fat-mouthing about Rapunzel's fate,
SAM had slipped inside his John. I opened the door of
carved griffins and gargoyles. There was the Great Commode! But I had no time to admire it. On the floor
encircling the bowl were SAM's discarded shirt, pants
and shoes. Footprints tracked the tile near the bowl.
Well, at least one print. The other was the mark of a
hoof covered with blotches of fresh dung. Had he disappeared into thin air?

I walked over to the bowl. There were heavy stains
on its sides as if some object had squeezed through
with much effort.

"I know where he is," I announced to the crowd,
some of whom had dispersed throughout the motel and
were helping themselves to SAM's legacy.

I ran up the stairs and out onto the path. Down
toward the statues of the Presidents I charged, trampling
twigs and cutting through the thicket. Some fingers were
creeping over the rim of one of the mouths as an uneven
flow of puslike substance roared into the Black Bay.

Then a gas mask peered out as SAM, coming out of
RBH's trap on his back, chinned himself headfirst on
the lips. I crawled out onto RBH's nose. It was a long
drop to the bay so I moved with caution. When I
reached the edge where the fingers gripped the lips
holding on for dear life—while I clung to the cracked
nostrils of the President—I kind of lost my cool and
stomped up a storm on my man's fingers.

"NO! NO! LET'S GOAT-SHE-ATE THIS THING."

But lightning struck his mask as the smashed fingers
slowly slipped from the rim of the lips. The gas mask
tore away as SAM fell back into the waters sending a

geyser of spray many miles high while ripples fanned
out across the waters sending tides to the banks of the
Emperor Franz Joseph Park. For one brief second as the
gas mask fell away from his face I caught a glimpse of
it.

NOW I WAS DA ONE. NOW NOT ONLY WOULD
I BE THE NAZARENE BISHOP WHICH WAS AFTER
ALL PEANUTS, BUT I WAS GOING TO RUN THE
WHOLE KIT AND KABOODLE. ME DICTATOR OF
BUKKA DOOPEYDUK. NOW DEY WOULD HAVE
TO PUT DEM JOOLED ANTLERS ON MY HEAD
AND NOW I WOULD BE DA ONE SURROUNDED
WITH DEM TENDENTS WHO WOULD WAIT ON
ME HAND AND FOOT AND EVERYONE DIDN'T
LIKE IT WOULD BE SLUGGED. HA HA HA HA
HA HA HA HA HA, DA GOLDEN BEDPAN WAS
MINE NOW AND I WOULD BE DA ONE GIVE
OUT DA BINGO SCORES, HAR HAR HAR.

I walked up the path toward my motel, exultant, re-
hearsing the phonemes of UNNERSTAND and INNER-
STEAD. I COMBED MY HAIR WITH A TWO-FOOT
COMB.

A noise came from inside the main ballroom where
people were running around the halls with their arms
loaded with SAM's legacy—locks of Roy Rogers' hair,
Picayune cartons, Hershey bars (semisweet and sweet
chocolate), spittoons, phonograph records, etc.

But the fourth door had been opened. Deep tracks
in the rug indicated that a massive object had been
rolled from the room and into the ballroom. I opened
the door of the ballroom. A giant smiling replica of
HARRY SAM in a squatting position had been brought
out. IT WAS WHITE HOT WITH ELECTRICITY! The

people were climbing into the molten-hot lap and whining at the top of their lungs.

"WAIT! WAIT! GET OUT DAT LAP! I'M DA ONE WHO'S BOSS! LISTEN TO ME."

On the other side of the room a familiar voice shouted, "STOP HIM! THAT'S THE ONE!"

I turned to see a battery of microphones and TV crews wheeling in and out. The next-in-rank on the Civil Service list was being sworn in. He was surrounded by fourteen of his followers; little men in quilted jackets. Nosetrouble was administering the oath and Cipher X was pointing an accusing finger at me. I started to cop a plea but found myself looking into the barrel of a gun held by one of the little men.

I was hung by meathooks in the Emperor Franz Joseph Park. It was televised nationally, narrated by Fredric March and written up in *Variety*. On the first day a weird boat moved up the bay. The entire student body and faculty of the University of Buffalo were riding behind on surfboards. They held hoopla hoops under their arms. They also carried some subscription blanks for the *Deformed Demokrat* (which incidentally had bought serial rights for U2 Polyglot's long-awaited paper). Two men leaning over the bank waved to me. They were Matthew and Waldo going into exile as guests of the mayor, Steve Wolinski. His honor stood next to them munching on a thirteen-foot kabalsa. Steve was overjoyed. Not only were there plenty of snowplows and cement in the boat's hold, but now he'll be the hit of the Chopin Singing Society with the news of all the BECOMINGS and avant-garde muggle-smoking and head trips going on in NOW-HERE.

On the second day of my swinging, I was visited

by my parents. They placed a gaudy wreath at my
feet, then made a request. "Bukka, we saw you on television and called up the television people to ask how
much time on the air cost. They said that television is
very expensive. Right, honey?"

"Right," answered my father, having added a Billy
Eckstine shirt to his items of adornment.

"We got the time chart to see how much air time
cost. Way we figure it, you must be cleaning up. We
were wondering whether you could turn us on to some
change so that we can add an air conditioner to the
sixth house we just bought to rent out."

"I didn't receive anything, mother. Do you think that
I enjoy swinging by these meathooks?"

"Nigger probably lying," my father said. "Soon as he
get famous he forget about his peoples. Well, as my
mother use to say before she flaked out, 'hard head
makes a soft ass.' Let's go, dear. The Donna Reed Show
is on the other channel. We'll fix him. We'll support his
competitor."

Just as they walked toward the subway Rapunzel came
up and placed a gift-wrapped box of Gillette razor blades
at my feet. I was touched. "I was on the way to Aqueduct
and I wanted to show you my 'preciation for sparing
me and to ask you a couple of pertinent questions. First
of all, how come you let me go?"

"The preacher said that you had stolen the secret of
the Black Bay from Matthew and Waldo and gave it
to him so that he might save us. Where did SAM get
ahold of the bottle that cleared the Black Bay, Rapunzel?"

"SAM thought that if things ever got hot, he'd have
to take it on the lam. Like if GOAT-SHE-ATE-SHUNS
failed or something. So he had the Counter Insurgency

Foundation invent this formula what would work if he ever had to swim the Black Bay. They worked closely with this ol dame who was corresponding—"

"O, no, no, no. That old witch again!" My father-in-law's mother would be the death of me yet.

"Well, anyway, Bukka, tanks again."

"Wait a minute, Rapunzel," I asked. "Why did you bother to save me?"

"I don't know. I ask myself that all the time. Why did I stick my neck out? Maybe it's because you had balls and most of the kats who came up there were always talking about SAM behind his back but when they were with him they were kissing his ass all the time. You stood up to the guy. Which reminds me," Rapunzel continued, "there was somethin' else puzzlin' me and it confused SAM too but he didn't say anything to you about it because he thought it was some special custom your people had, and didn't want to seem ignorant about it. What was that Nazareeny thing you kept yapping about?"

"Well, Rapunzel, it's a long story," I began. "It all started when I stood outside my dean's office when he was pushing this ball of manure around the world by his nose. . . . I mean, you see, these kids were on an elevator one day fighting with clipboards and they disappeared. . . . You see, there was this thing stuck in my frig and it asked could I arrange an appointment for it with SAM. . . . O, no, that's not the way. What's the use?" I said, giving up the ghost, as the little man removed his derby and bowed his head.

On the night of the third day, the darkness surrounding out-of-sight became a horrifying yellow. Hundreds of eye-holes encircled NOW-HERE. It was the Free-Lance Pallbearers. (Better late den never.) They had come to cut me down. But you see they couldn't get through. There was this great ball of manure suspended above Klang-a-Lang-a-Ding-Dong. Held down by spikes and rope it stank to high heaven. The Pallbearers consulted the maps provided by the martyred neighbor's son and his sidekick, Joel O. A little figure hobbled on crutches moving through these deadly professionals. It was U2 Polyglot making his way toward a mailbox behind the Free-Lance Pallbearers. His arm was in a sling. He had been winged while U-twoing through Indochina but nothing can stand in the way of scholarship.

So he dropped the greenish-brown envelope containing his manuscript into the mail. He sat down to contemplate his next paper. It was a beautiful night and U2 lit up a pipe and marveled at the motel standing on the mountain, across the bay. Helicopters bounced up and down on its roof and the sign of the new regime blinked on and off:

EATS–SAVE GREEN STAMPS–BINGO–WED–EATS–SAVE GREEN STAMPS–BINGO–WED–EATS–SAVE GREEN STAMPS–BINGO–WED–EATS–SAVE GREEN STAMPS–BINGO–WED–EATS–SAVE

WRITTEN IN CHINESE   NO LESS

Aug. 13, 1966,
HELL'S Kitchen, New York

DALKEY ARCHIVE PAPERBACKS

YUZ ALESHKOVSKY, *Kangaroo*.
FELIPE ALFAU, *Chromos*.
  Locos.
  Sentimental Songs.
ALAN ANSEN,
  Contact Highs: Selected Poems 1957-1987.
DJUNA BARNES, *Ladies Almanack*.
  Ryder.
JOHN BARTH, *LETTERS*.
  Sabbatical.
ANDREI BITOV, *Pushkin House*.
ROGER BOYLAN, *Killoyle*.
CHRISTINE BROOKE-ROSE, *Amalgamemnon*.
GERALD BURNS, *Shorter Poems*.
GABRIELLE BURTON, *Heartbreak Hotel*.
MICHEL BUTOR,
  Portrait of the Artist as a Young Ape.
JULIETA CAMPOS,
  The Fear of Losing Eurydice.
ANNE CARSON, *Eros the Bittersweet*.
LOUIS-FERDINAND CÉLINE, *Castle to Castle*.
  London Bridge.
  North.
  Rigadoon.
HUGO CHARTERIS, *The Tide Is Right*.
JEROME CHARYN, *The Tar Baby*.
EMILY HOLMES COLEMAN,
  The Shutter of Snow.
ROBERT COOVER, *A Night at the Movies*.
STANLEY CRAWFORD,
  Some Instructions to My Wife.
RENÉ CREVEL, *Putting My Foot in It*.
RALPH CUSACK, *Cadenza*.
SUSAN DAITCH, *Storytown*.
PETER DIMOCK,
  A Short Rhetoric for Leaving the Family.
COLEMAN DOWELL, *Island People*.
  Too Much Flesh and Jabez.
RIKKI DUCORNET, *The Complete Butcher's Tales*.
  The Fountains of Neptune.
  The Jade Cabinet.
  Phosphor in Dreamland.
  The Stain.
WILLIAM EASTLAKE, *Castle Keep*.
  Lyric of the Circle Heart.

STANLEY ELKIN, *Boswell: A Modern Comedy*.
  The Dick Gibson Show.
  The MacGuffin.
ANNIE ERNAUX, *Cleaned Out*.
LAUREN FAIRBANKS, *Muzzle Thyself*.
  Sister Carrie.
LESLIE A. FIEDLER,
  Love and Death in the American Novel.
RONALD FIRBANK, *Complete Short Stories*.
FORD MADOX FORD, *The March of Literature*.
JANICE GALLOWAY, *Foreign Parts*.
  The Trick Is to Keep Breathing.
WILLIAM H. GASS, *The Tunnel*.
  Willie Masters' Lonesome Wife.
C. S. GISCOMBE, *Giscome Road*.
  Here.
KAREN ELIZABETH GORDON, *The Red Shoes*.
PATRICK GRAINVILLE, *The Cave of Heaven*.
GEOFFREY GREEN, ET AL, *The Vineland Papers*.
JIŘÍ GRUŠA, *The Questionnaire*.
JOHN HAWKES, *Whistlejacket*.
ALDOUS HUXLEY, *Antic Hay*.
  Point Counter Point.
  Those Barren Leaves.
  Time Must Have a Stop.
GERT JONKE, *Geometric Regional Novel*.
TADEUSZ KONWICKI, *A Minor Apocalypse*.
  The Polish Complex.
EWA KURYLUK, *Century 21*.
DEBORAH LEVY, *Billy and Girl*.
JOSÉ LEZAMA LIMA, *Paradiso*.
OSMAN LINS, *The Queen of the Prisons of Greece*.
ALF MAC LOCHLAINN,
  The Corpus in the Library.
  Out of Focus.
D. KEITH MANO, *Take Five*.
BEN MARCUS, *The Age of Wire and String*.
WALLACE MARKFIELD, *Teitlebaum's Window*.
DAVID MARKSON, *Collected Poems*.
  Reader's Block.
  Springer's Progress.
  Wittgenstein's Mistress.
CARL R. MARTIN, *Genii Over Salzburg*.
CAROLE MASO, *AVA*.
HARRY MATHEWS, *Cigarettes*.

Visit our website: www.dalkeyarchive.com

🔲
DALKEY ARCHIVE PAPERBACKS

The Conversions.
The Journalist.
The Sinking of the Odradek Stadium.
Singular Pleasures.
Tlooth.
20 Lines a Day.
JOSEPH MCELROY, Women and Men.
ROBERT L. MCLAUGHLIN, ED.,
  Innovations: An Anthology of Modern &
  Contemporary Fiction.
JAMES MERRILL, The (Diblos) Notebook.
STEVEN MILLHAUSER, The Barnum Museum.
  In the Penny Arcade.
OLIVE MOORE, Spleen.
STEVEN MOORE, Ronald Firbank: An Annotated
  Bibliography.
NICHOLAS MOSLEY, Accident.
  Assassins.
  Children of Darkness and Light.
  Impossible Object.
  Judith.
  Natalie Natalia.
WARREN F. MOTTE, JR., Oulipo.
YVES NAVARRE, Our Share of Time.
WILFRIDO D. NOLLEDO, But for the Lovers.
FLANN O'BRIEN, At Swim-Two-Birds.
  The Best of Myles.
  The Dalkey Archive.
  The Hard Life.
  The Poor Mouth.
  The Third Policeman.
CLAUDE OLLIER, The Mise-en-Scène.
FERNANDO DEL PASO, Palinuro of Mexico.
RAYMOND QUENEAU, The Last Days.
  Pierrot Mon Ami.
  Saint Glinglin.
ISHMAEL REED, The Free-Lance Pallbearers.
  The Terrible Twos.
  The Terrible Threes.
REYOUNG, Unbabbling.
JULIÁN RÍOS, Poundemonium.
JACQUES ROUBAUD, Some Thing Black.
  The Great Fire of London.
  The Plurality of Worlds of Lewis.

The Princess Hoppy.
LEON S. ROUDIEZ, French Fiction Revisited.
SEVERO SARDUY, Cobra and Maitreya.
ARNO SCHMIDT, Collected Stories.
  Nobodaddy's Children.
JUNE AKERS SEESE,
  Is This What Other Women Feel Too?
  What Waiting Really Means.
VIKTOR SHKLOVSKY, Theory of Prose.
JOSEF SKVORECKY,
  The Engineer of Human Souls.
CLAUDE SIMON, The Invitation.
GILBERT SORRENTINO, Aberration of Starlight.
  Crystal Vision.
  Imaginative Qualities of Actual Things.
  Mulligan Stew.
  Pack of Lies.
  The Sky Changes.
  Splendide-Hôtel.
  Steelwork.
  Under the Shadow.
W. M. SPACKMAN, The Complete Fiction.
GERTRUDE STEIN, The Making of Americans.
  A Novel of Thank You.
PIOTR SZEWC, Annihilation.
ALEXANDER THEROUX, The Lollipop Trollops.
ESTHER TUSQUETS, Stranded.
LUISA VALENZUELA, He Who Searches.
PAUL WEST,
  Words for a Deaf Daughter and Gala.
CURTIS WHITE,
  Memories of My Father Watching TV.
  Monstrous Possibility.
DIANE WILLIAMS,
  Excitability: Selected Stories.
DOUGLAS WOOLF, Wall to Wall.
PHILIP WYLIE, Generation of Vipers.
MARGUERITE YOUNG, Angel in the Forest.
  Miss MacIntosh, My Darling.
LOUIS ZUKOFSKY, Collected Fiction.
SCOTT ZWIREN, God Head.

Visit our website: www.dalkeyarchive.com
Dalkey Archive Press
ISU Campus Box 4241, Normal, IL 61790–4241
fax (309) 438–7422